BURN1NG
CHROME

An Imprint of HarperCollins*Publishers*

WILLIAM GIBSON

BURNING CHROME

"Johnny Mnemonic"; "Hinterlands"; "Red Star, Winter Orbit"; "New Rose Hotel"; "Dogfight"; and "Burning Chrome" © by Omni Publication International Ltd., 1981, 1982, 1983, 1985. "The Gernsback Continuum" first appeared in *Universe 11,* © 1981 by Terry Carr. "Fragments of a Hologram Rose" © 1977 by UnEarth Publications. "The Belonging Kind" first appeared in *Shadows 4,* © 1981 by John Shirley and William Gibson.

This book was originally published in hardcover by Arbor House Publishing Company in 1986 and in a mass market edition by Ace Books in 1987.

HarperCollins books may be purchased for educational, business, or sales promotional use. For information, please e-mail the Special Markets Depart-Department at SPsales@harpercollins.com.

First Eos paperback edition published 2003.

Designed by Nicola Ferguson

Library of Congress Cataloging-in-Publication Data
Gibson, William, 1948–
Burning chrome / William Gibson.—1st. EOS trade pbk. ed.
p. cm.
Originally published: New York: Arbor House, c1986. With new introduction.
ISBN 0-06-053982-8
1. Science fiction, American. I. Title.
PS3557.I2264B875 2003
813'.54—dc21   2003040619

24 25 26 27 28 LBC 27 26 25 24 23

To Otey Williams Gibson,
my mother, and to Mildred Barnitz,
her true dear friend and mine, with love

Contents

by Bruce Sterling

i f poets are the unacknowledged legislators of the world, science-fiction writers are its court jesters. We are Wise Fools who can leap, caper, utter prophecies, and scratch ourselves in public. We can play with Big Ideas because the garish motley of our pulp origins makes us seem harmless.

And SF writers have every opportunity to kick up our heels—we have influence without responsibility. Very few feel obliged to take us seriously, yet our ideas permeate the culture, bubbling along invisibly, like background radiation.

Yet the sad truth of the matter is that SF has not been much fun of late. All forms of pop culture go through doldrums; they catch cold when society sneezes. If SF in the late Seventies was confused, self-involved, and stale, it was scarcely a cause for wonder.

But William Gibson is one of our best harbingers of better things to come.

His brief career has already established him as a definitive Eighties writer. His amazing first novel, *Neuromancer*, which swept the field's awards in 1985, showed Gibson's unparalleled ability to pinpoint social nerves. The effect was galvanic, helping to wake the genre from its dogmatic slumbers. Roused from its hibernation, SF is lurching from its cave into the bright sunlight of the modern zeitgeist. And we are lean and hungry and not in the best of tempers. From now on things are going to be different.

The collection you hold now contains all of Gibson's shorter work to date. It's a rare chance to see the astonishingly rapid development of a major writer.

The tack he intended to take was already visible in his first published story, "Fragments of a Hologram Rose," from 1977. The Gibson trademarks are already present: a complex synthesis of modern pop culture, high tech, and advanced literary technique.

Gibson's second story, "The Gernsback Continuum," shows him consciously drawing a bead on the shambling figure of the SF tradition. It's a devastating refutation of "scientifiction" in its guise as narrow technolatry. We see here a writer who knows his roots and is gearing up for a radical reformation.

Gibson hit his stride with the Sprawl series: "Johnny Mnemonic," "New Rose Hotel," and the incredible "Burning Chrome." The appearance of these stories in *Omni* magazine showed a level of imaginative concentration that effectively upped the ante for the entire genre. These densely packed, baroque stories repay several readings for their hard-edged, gloomy passion and intensely realized detail.

The triumph of these pieces was their brilliant, self-consistent evocation of a credible future. It is hard to over-estimate the difficulty of this effort, which is one that many SF writers have been ducking for years. This intellectual failing accounts for the ominous proliferation of postapocalypse stories, sword-and-sorcery fantasies, and those everpresent space operas in which galactic empires slip conveniently back into barbarism. All these subgenres are products of the writers' urgent necessity to avoid tangling with a realistic future.

But in the Sprawl stories we see a future that is recognizably and painstakingly drawn from the modern condition. It is multifaceted, sophisticated, global in its view. It derives from a new set of starting points: not from the shopworn formula of robots, spaceships, and the modern miracle of atomic energy, but from cybernetics, biotech, and the communications web— to name a few.

Gibson's extrapolative techniques are those of classic hard SF, but his demonstration of them is pure New Wave. Rather than the usual passionless techies and rock-ribbed Competent Men of hard SF, his characters are a pirate's crew of losers, hustlers, spin-offs, castoffs, and lunatics. We see his future from the belly up, as it is lived, not merely as dry speculation.

Gibson puts an end to that fertile Gernsbackian archetype, Ralph 124C41+, a white-bread technocrat in his ivory tower, who showers the blessings of super-science upon the hoi polloi. In Gibson's work we find ourselves in the streets and alleys, in a realm of sweaty, white-knuckled survival, where high tech is a constant subliminal hum, "like a deranged experiment in social Darwinism, designed by a bored researcher who kept one thumb permanently on the fast-forward button."

Big Science in this world is not a source of quaint Mr. Wizard marvels, but an omnipresent, all-permeating, definitive force. It is a sheet of mutating radiation pouring through a crowd, a jam-packed Global Bus roaring wildly up an exponential slope.

These stories paint an instantly recognizable portrait of the modern predicament. Gibson's extrapolations show, with exaggerated clarity, the hidden bulk of an iceberg of social change. This iceberg now glides with sinister majesty across the surface of the late twentieth century, but its proportions are vast and dark.

Many SF authors, faced with this lurking monster, have flung up their hands and predicted shipwreck. Though no one could accuse Gibson of Pollyannaism, he has avoided this easy out. This is another distinguishing mark of the emergent new

school of Eighties SF: its boredom with the Apocalypse. Gibson
wastes very little time shaking his finger or wringing his hands.
He keeps his eyes unflinchingly open and, as Algis Budrys has
pointed out, he is not afraid of hard work. These are signal
virtues.

Another sign shows Gibson as part of a growing new con-
sensus in SF: the ease with which he collaborates with other
writers. Three such collaborations grace this collection. "The
Belonging Kind" is a rare treat, a dark fantasy bubbling over
with lunatic surrealism. "Red Star, Winter Orbit" is another
near-future piece with a lovingly detailed, authentic, background; with the global, multicultural point of view typical of
Eighties SF. "Dogfight" is a savagely effective and brutally
twisted piece of work, with Gibson's classic one-two combination of lowlife and high tech.

In Gibson we hear the sound of a decade that has finally
found its own voice. He is not a table-pounding revolutionary,
but a practical, hands-on retrofitter. He is opening the stale
corridors of the genre to the fresh air of new data: Eighties culture, with its strange, growing integration of technology and
fashion. He has a fondness for the odder and more inventive
byways of mainstream lit: Le Carré, Robert Stone, Pynchon,
William Burroughs, Jayne Anne Phillips. And he is a devotee of
what J. G. Ballard has perceptively called "invisible literature":
that permeating flow of scientific reports, government docu-
ments, and specialized advertising that shapes our culture
below the level of recognition.

SF has survived a long winter on its stored body fat. Gibson,
along with a broad wave of inventive, ambitious new writers, has
prodded the genre awake and sent it out on recce for a fresh
diet. And it's bound to do us all a power of good.

by William Gibson

nothing acquires quite as rapid or peculiar a patina of age as an imaginary future.

As a boy in the 1960s, I read a great deal of science fiction, much of it written in the 1940s and 1950s. This actually forced me to decode, early on, some fairly major elements of modern history, if only because one can't really enjoy what science fiction does without being able to recognize the point at which the imaginary lifts off from the known.

But history, I've since come to believe, is the ultimate in speculative narrative, subject to ongoing and inevitable revision.

Science fiction tends to behave like a species of history pointing in the opposite direction, up the timeline rather than back. But you can't draw imaginary future histories without a map of the past that your readers will accept as their own.

The less you think your map of the past imaginary (or contingent), the more conventionally you tend to stride forward into your imaginary future. Many of the authors I read as a boy possessed remarkably solid maps of the past. Carved, it seemed, from doughty oak. Confident men, they knew exactly where we were coming from, exactly where we were, and exactly where they thought we were going. And they were largely wrong on all three counts, at least as seen from this much farther up the tracks.

But there was another, variant species of science fiction, unnamed but to my mind somehow distinct, which seemed to start from less fixed assumptions of history, a fiction whose writers seemed willing to entertain ideas that suggested we might, in fact, not know where we'd come from, or even where we were—that we were perhaps failing to recognize where we were for what it most basically was.

Alfred Bester, Fritz Leiber, Robert Sheckley (to name only three, but very fine, examples) all did this for me, whereas Heinlein and Asimov didn't. The writers who made science fiction do what for me was its most magic thing seemed to inhabit a more urban universe, a universe with more moving parts, one in which more questions could be asked (if far fewer definitively answered). These writers were somehow in a different relationship to what I would learn, later, to call "the Modern."

By the time I came to be writing the stories in this collection, in my own mid-twenties, in the 1980s, cultural models of modernity were starting to lose resolution. The dissatisfactions I brought to their writing, the burrs under the saddle of my early method, had to do with some sense of that—of the Modern starting to suffer from bit rot, and from a conviction that science fiction hadn't quite been doing its best job about that. Or perhaps more fairly that most science fiction seemed seldom to be doing that which I personally most enjoyed it doing, in spite of what seemed to me to be a host of entirely new and wonderful opportunities.

But if you'd asked me to define what it was, exactly, that I wanted science fiction to be doing, I probably couldn't have told you. Being as constitutionally incapable of theory as I was of criticism, all I could do was write these stories.

Which I didn't, as a glance at the table of contents shows, always do entirely on my own. For those committed to the auteur theory of literature, no excuse will suffice here, but for the rest of you I simply make the point that I evidently wasn't alone in my dissatisfaction.

The source code for these stories was compiled in equal measure from the dissatisfaction mentioned above, from a childhood that had exposed me simultaneously to science fiction and the Beats (mainly Burroughs and Kerouac), and from my personal association with writers on the order of Sterling, Shirley, and Swanwick, all of whom had burrs, not dissimilar, under their respective saddles. Had any one of these three factors been lacking, you probably wouldn't be reading this introduction.

"Fragments of a Hologram Rose," the first piece of fiction I ever managed to complete, was written in lieu of a term paper for a course in science fiction taught by the late Dr. Susan Wood at the University of British Columbia in 1977. "The Gernsback Continuum" actually began as a long review of an illustrated history of the streamlined Moderne, which was promptly rejected by a science fiction fanzine as being bafflingly off-topic. "The Belonging Kind" was my uninvited attempt at rewriting a John Shirley manuscript, the ultimate in longhand criticism and the only kind I was capable of, with John turning the tables on me by promptly selling it as our collaboration. "Johnny Mnemonic" was the second piece of fiction I ever attempted, beginning in 1977 and finishing in 1981 (I had paused to observe, as an age-designated noncombatant, the phenomenon of punk rock, which also has its place in the source code). "Dogfight" began with my telling someone of my hypnagogic vision of miniature biplanes flying inches above a pool table; they mentioned this to Swanwick, who shortly phoned from Philadelphia to announce that he'd worked out the technological rationale to a nicety (an extremely dreamlike start to a collaboration). "Red

Star, Winter Orbit" was proposed, I'm sure, by the endlessly energetic Sterling, who would later, with identical enthusiasm, suggest that we write a very long novel together about steam-driven Victorian computers, my experience of "Red Star" predisposing me to not instantly run away screaming.

"Burning Chrome," written in early 1981, feels to me now like the end of my career in short fiction. It wasn't, chronologically (and short fiction is something I perpetually hope to take up again, eventually), but it was in some way the real start of my career as a novelist. Within it gun the engines of *Neuromancer,* and not only in its introduction of "cyberspace," a word that first saw the light in red Sharpie on a yellow legal pad. It was the first time I ever quite got something else to work in fiction, though I still don't know exactly what that is.

It's been argued that "the single" (a one-cut vinyl recording in either 78 or 45 rpm format) was the medium that defined the most perfect expressions of rock: that the single is in fact that music's optimal form. The same has sometimes been said of the short story and science fiction. In the case of rock, I'm inclined to suspect nostalgia for a dead media platform. In the case of science fiction, I think there may be something to it. It requires a very peculiar sort of literary musculature to write a very short piece of science fiction that really works.

If I ever did that, you'll find it here.

In any case, enjoy the patina.

October 21, 2002

BURN1NG
CHROME

i put the shotgun in an Adidas bag and padded it out with four pairs of tennis socks, not my style at all, but that was what I was aiming for: If they think you're crude, go technical; if they think you're technical, go crude. I'm a very technical boy. So I decided to get as crude as possible. These days, though, you have to be pretty technical before you can even aspire to crudeness. I'd had to turn both these twelve-gauge shells from brass stock, on a lathe, and then load them myself; I'd had to dig up an old microfiche with instructions for hand-loading cartridges; I'd had to build a lever-action press to seat the primers—all very tricky. But I knew they'd work.

The meet was set for the Drome at 2300, but I rode the tube three stops past the closest platform and walked back. Immaculate procedure.

I checked myself out in the chrome siding of a coffee kiosk, your basic sharp-faced Caucasoid with a ruff of stiff, dark hair. The girls at Under the Knife were big on Sony Mao, and it was getting harder to keep them from adding the chic suggestion of epicanthic folds. It probably wouldn't fool Ralfi Face, but it might get me next to his table.

The Drome is a single narrow space with a bar down one side and tables along the other, thick with pimps and handlers and an arcane array of dealers. The Magnetic Dog Sisters were on the door that night, and I didn't relish trying to get out past them if things didn't work out. They were two meters tall and thin as greyhounds. One was black and the other white, but aside from that they were as nearly identical as cosmetic surgery could make them. They'd been lovers for years and were bad news in a tussle. I was never quite sure which one had originally been male.

Ralfi was sitting at his usual table. Owing me a lot of money. I had hundreds of megabytes stashed in my head on an idiot/savant basis, information I had no conscious access to. Ralfi had left it there. He hadn't, however, come back for it. Only Ralfi could retrieve the data, with a code phrase of his own invention. I'm not cheap to begin with, but my overtime on storage is astronomical. And Ralfi had been very scarce.

Then I'd heard that Ralfi Face wanted to put out a contract on me. So I'd arranged to meet him in the Drome, but I'd arranged it as Edward Bax, clandestine importer, late of Rio and Peking.

The Drome stank of biz, a metallic tang of nervous tension. Muscle-boys scattered through the crowd were flexing stock parts at one another and trying on thin, cold grins, some of them so lost under superstructures of muscle graft that their outlines weren't really human.

Pardon me. Pardon me, friends. Just Eddie Bax here, Fast Eddie the Importer, with his professionally nondescript gym bag, and please ignore this slit, just wide enough to admit his right hand.

Ralfi wasn't alone. Eighty kilos of blond California beef perched alertly in the chair next to his, martial arts written all over him.

Fast Eddie Bax was in the chair opposite them before the beef's hands were off the table. "You black belt?" I asked eagerly. He nodded, blue eyes running an automatic scanning pattern between my eyes and my hands. "Me, too," I said. "Got mine here in the bag." And I shoved my hand through the slit and thumbed the safety off. Click. "Double twelve-gauge with the triggers wired together."

"That's a gun," Ralfi said, putting a plump, restraining hand on his boy's taut blue nylon chest. "Johnny has an antique firearm in his bag." So much for Edward Bax.

I guess he'd always been Ralfi Something or Other, but he owed his acquired surname to a singular vanity. Built something like an overripe pear, he'd worn the once-famous face of Christian White for twenty years—Christian White of the Aryan Reggae Band, Sony Mao to his generation, and final champion of race rock. I'm a whiz at trivia.

Christian White: classic pop face with a singer's high-definition muscles, chiseled cheekbones. Angelic in one light, handsomely depraved in another. But Ralfi's eyes lived behind that face, and they were small and cold and black.

"Please," he said, "let's work this out like businessmen." His voice was marked by a horrible prehensile sincerity, and the corners of his beautiful Christian White mouth were always wet. "Lewis here," nodding in the beefboy's direction, "is a meatball." Lewis took this impassively, looking like something built from a kit. "You aren't a meatball, Johnny."

"Sure I am, Ralfi, a nice meatball chock-full of implants where you can store your dirty laundry while you go off shopping for people to kill me. From my end of this bag, Ralfi, it looks like you've got some explaining to do."

"It's this last batch of product, Johnny." He sighed deeply. "In my role as broker—"

"Fence," I corrected.

"As broker, I'm usually very careful as to sources."

"You buy only from those who steal the best. Got it."

He sighed again. "I try," he said wearily, "not to buy from

fools. This time, I'm afraid, I've done that." Third sigh was the cue for Lewis to trigger the neural disruptor they'd taped under my side of the table.

I put everything I had into curling the index finger of my right hand, but I no longer seemed to be connected to it. I could feel the metal of the gun and the foam-pad tape I'd wrapped around the stubby grip, but my hands were cool wax, distant and inert. I was hoping Lewis was a true meatball, thick enough to go for the gym bag and snag my rigid trigger finger, but he wasn't.

"We've been very worried about you, Johnny. Very worried. You see, that's Yakuza property you have there. A fool took it from them, Johnny. A dead fool."

Lewis giggled.

It all made sense then, an ugly kind of sense, like bags of wet sand settling around my head. Killing wasn't Ralfi's style. Lewis wasn't even Ralfi's style. But he'd got himself stuck between the Sons of the Neon Chrysanthemum and something that belonged to them—or, more likely, something of theirs that belonged to someone else. Ralfi, of course, could use the code phrase to throw me into idiot/savant, and I'd spill their hot program without remembering a single quarter tone. For a fence like Ralfi, that would ordinarily have been enough. But not for the Yakuza. The Yakuza would know about Squids, for one thing, and they wouldn't want to worry about one lifting those dim and permanent traces of their program out of my head. I didn't know very much about Squids, but I'd heard stories, and I made it a point never to repeat them to my clients. No, the Yakuza wouldn't like that; it looked too much like evidence. They hadn't got where they were by leaving evidence around. Or alive.

Lewis was grinning. I think he was visualizing a point just behind my forehead and imagining how he could get there the hard way.

"Hey," said a low voice, feminine, from somewhere behind my right shoulder, "you cowboys sure aren't having too lively a time."

"Pack it, bitch," Lewis said, his tanned face very still. Ralfi looked blank.

"Lighten up. You want to buy some good free base?" She pulled up a chair and quickly sat before either of them could stop her. She was barely inside my fixed field of vision, a thin girl with mirrored glasses, her dark hair cut in a rough shag. She wore black leather, open over a T-shirt slashed diagonally with stripes of red and black. "Eight thou a gram weight."

Lewis snorted his exasperation and tried to slap her out of the chair. Somehow he didn't quite connect, and her hand came up and seemed to brush his wrist as it passed. Bright blood sprayed the table. He was clutching his wrist white-knuckle tight, blood trickling from between his fingers.

But hadn't her hand been empty?

He was going to need a tendon stapler. He stood up carefully, without bothering to push his chair back. The chair toppled backward, and he stepped out of my line of sight without a word.

"He better get a medic to look at that," she said. "That's a nasty cut."

"You have no idea," said Ralfi, suddenly sounding very tired, "the depths of shit you have just gotten yourself into."

"No kidding? Mystery. I get real excited by mysteries. Like why your friend here's so quiet. Frozen, like. Or what this thing here is for," and she held up the little control unit that she'd somehow taken from Lewis. Ralfi looked ill.

"You, ah, want maybe a quarter-million to give me that and take a walk?" A fat hand came up to stroke his pale, lean face nervously.

"What I want," she said, snapping her fingers so that the unit spun and glittered, "is work. A job. Your boy hurt his wrist. But a quarter'll do for a retainer."

Ralfi let his breath out explosively and began to laugh, exposing teeth that hadn't been kept up to the Christian White standard. Then she turned the disruptor off.

"Two million," I said.

"My kind of man," she said, and laughed. "What's in the bag?"

"A shotgun."

"Crude." It might have been a compliment.

Ralfi said nothing at all.

"Name's Millions. Molly Millions. You want to get out of here, boss? People are starting to stare." She stood up. She was wearing leather jeans the color of dried blood.

And I saw for the first time that the mirrored lenses were surgical inlays, the silver rising smoothly from her high cheekbones, sealing her eyes in their sockets. I saw my new face twinned there.

"I'm Johnny," I said. "We're taking Mr. Face with us."

he was outside, waiting. Looking like your standard tourist tech, in plastic zoris and a silly Hawaiian shirt printed with blowups of his firm's most popular micro-processor; a mild little guy, the kind most likely to wind up drunk on sake in a bar that puts out miniature rice crackers with seaweed garnish. He looked like the kind who sing the corporate anthem and cry, who shake hands endlessly with the bartender. And the pimps and the dealers would leave him alone, pegging him as innately conservative. Not up for much, and careful with his credit when he was.

The way I figured it later, they must have amputated part of his left thumb, somewhere behind the first joint, replacing it with a prosthetic tip, and cored the stump, fitting it with a spool and socket molded from one of the Ono-Sendai diamond analogs. Then they'd carefully wound the spool with three meters of monomolecular filament.

Molly got into some kind of exchange with the Magnetic Dog Sisters, giving me a chance to usher Ralfi through the door with the gym bag pressed lightly against the base of his spine. She seemed to know them. I heard the black one laugh.

I glanced up, out of some passing reflex, maybe because I've never got used to it, to the soaring arcs of light and the shadows of the geodesics above them. Maybe that saved me.

Ralfi kept walking, but I don't think he was trying to escape. I think he'd already given up. Probably he already had an idea of what we were up against.

I looked back down in time to see him explode.

Playback on full recall shows Ralfi stepping forward as the little tech sidles out of nowhere, smiling. Just a suggestion of a bow, and his left thumb falls off. It's a conjuring trick. The thumb hangs suspended. Mirrors? Wires? And Ralfi stops, his back to us, dark crescents of sweat under the armpits of his pale summer suit. He knows. He must have known. And then the joke-shop thumbtip, heavy as lead, arcs out in a lightning yo-yo trick, and the invisible thread connecting it to the killer's hand passes laterally through Ralfi's skull, just above his eyebrows, whips up, and descends, slicing the pear-shaped torso diagonally from shoulder to rib cage. Cuts so fine that no blood flows until synapses misfire and the first tremors surrender the body to gravity.

Ralfi tumbled apart in a pink cloud of fluids, the three mismatched sections rolling forward onto the tiled pavement. In total silence.

I brought the gym bag up, and my hand convulsed. The recoil nearly broke my wrist.

it must have been raining; ribbons of water cascaded from a ruptured geodesic and spattered on the tile behind us. We crouched in the narrow gap between a surgical boutique and an antique shop. She'd just edged one mirrored eye around the corner to report a single Volks module in front of the Drome, red lights flashing. They were sweeping Ralfi up. Asking questions.

I was covered in scorched white fluff. The tennis socks. The gym bag was a ragged plastic cuff around my wrist. "I don't see how the hell I missed him."

" 'Cause he's fast, so fast." She hugged her knees and rocked back and forth on her bootheels. "His nervous system's jacked up. He's factory custom." She grinned and gave a little squeal of delight. "I'm gonna get that boy. Tonight. He's the best, number one, top dollar, state of the art."

"What you're going to get, for this boy's two million, is my ass out of here. Your boyfriend back there was mostly grown in a vat in Chiba City. He's a Yakuza assassin."

"Chiba. Yeah. See, Molly's been Chiba, too." And she showed me her hands, fingers slightly spread. Her fingers were slender, tapered, very white against the polished burgundy nails. Ten blades snicked straight out from their recesses beneath her nails, each one a narrow, double-edged scalpel in pale blue steel.

i'd never spent much time in Nighttown. Nobody there had anything to pay me to remember, and most of them had a lot they paid regularly to forget. Generations of sharpshooters had chipped away at the neon until the maintenance crews gave up. Even at noon the arcs were soot-black against faintest pearl.

Where do you go when the world's wealthiest criminal order is feeling for you with calm, distant fingers? Where do you hide from the Yakuza, so powerful that it owns comsats and at least three shuttles? The Yakuza is a true multinational, like ITT and Ono-Sendai. Fifty years before I was born the Yakuza had already absorbed the Triads, the Mafia, the Union Corse.

Molly had an answer: you hide in the Pit, in the lowest circle, where any outside influence generates swift, concentric ripples of raw menace. You hide in Nighttown. Better yet, you hide *above* Nighttown, because the Pit's inverted, and the bottom of its bowl touches the sky, the sky that Nighttown never sees, sweating under its own firmament of acrylic resin, up where the Lo Teks crouch in the dark like gargoyles, black-market cigarettes dangling from their lips.

She had another answer, too.

"So you're locked up good and tight, Johnny-san? No way to get that program without the password?" She led me into the shadows that waited beyond the bright tube platform. The concrete walls were overlaid with graffiti, years of them twisting into a single metascrawl of rage and frustration.

"The stored data are fed in through a modified series of microsurgical contraautism prostheses." I reeled off a numb version of my standard sales pitch. "Client's code is stored in a special chip; barring Squids, which we in the trade don't like to talk about, there's no way to recover your phrase. Can't drug it out, cut it out, torture it. I don't *know* it, never did."

"Squids? Crawly things with arms?" We emerged into a deserted street market. Shadowy figures watched us from across a makeshift square littered with fish heads and rotting fruit.

"Superconducting quantum interference detectors. Used them in the war to find submarines, suss out enemy cyber systems."

"Yeah? Navy stuff? From the war? Squid'll read that chip of yours?" She'd stopped walking, and I felt her eyes on me behind those twin mirrors.

"Even the primitive models could measure a magnetic field a billionth the strength of geomagnetic force; it's like pulling a whisper out of a cheering stadium."

"Cops can do that already, with parabolic microphones and lasers."

"But your data's still secure." Pride in profession. "No government'll let their cops have Squids, not even the security heavies. Too much chance of interdepartmental funnies; they're too likely to watergate you."

"Navy stuff," she said, and her grin gleamed in the shadows. "Navy stuff. I got a friend down here who was in the navy, name's Jones. I think you'd better meet him. He's a junkie, though. So we'll have to take him something."

"A junkie?"

"A dolphin."

he was more than a dolphin, but from another dolphin's point of view he might have seemed like something less. I watched him swirling sluggishly in his galvanized tank. Water slopped over the side, wetting my shoes. He was surplus from the last war. A cyborg.

He rose out of the water, showing us the crusted plates along his sides, a kind of visual pun, his grace nearly lost under articulated armor, clumsy and prehistoric. Twin deformities on either side of his skull had been engineered to house sensor units.

Silver lesions gleamed on exposed sections of his gray-white hide.

Molly whistled. Jones thrashed his tail, and more water cascaded down the side of the tank.

"What is this place?" I peered at vague shapes in the dark, rusting chain link and things under tarps. Above the tank hung a clumsy wooden framework, crossed and recrossed by rows of dusty Christmas lights.

"Funland. Zoo and carnival rides. 'Talk with the War Whale.' All that. Some whale Jones is. . . ."

Jones reared again and fixed me with a sad and ancient eye.

"How's he talk?" Suddenly I was anxious to go.

"That's the catch. Say 'hi,' Jones."

And all the bulbs lit simultaneously. They were flashing red, white, and blue.

RWBRWBRWB
RWBRWBRWB
RWBRWBRWB
RWBRWBRWB
RWBRWBRWB

"Good with symbols, see, but the code's restricted. In the navy they had him wired into an audiovisual display." She drew the narrow package from a jacket pocket. "Pure shit, Jones. Want it?" He froze in the water and started to sink. I felt a strange panic, remembering that he wasn't a fish, that he could drown. "We want the key to Johnny's bank, Jones. We want it fast."

The lights flickered, died.

"Go for it, Jones!"

```
            B
      BBBBBBBBB
            B
            B
            B
```

Blue bulbs, cruciform.

Darkness.

"Pure! It's *clean*. Come on, Jones."

```
      WWWWWWWWW
      WWWWWWWWW
      WWWWWWWWW
      WWWWWWWWW
      WWWWWWWWW
```

White sodium glare washed her features, stark mono-chrome, shadows cleaving from her cheekbones.

```
      R     RRRRR
      R     R
      RRRRRRRRR
            R     R
      RRRR     R
```

The arms of the red swastika were twisted in her silver glasses. "Give it to him," I said. "We've got it."

Ralfi Face. No imagination.

Jones heaved half his armored bulk over the edge of his tank, and I thought the metal would give way. Molly stabbed him overhand with the Syrette, driving the needle between two plates. Propellant hissed. Patterns of light exploded, spasming across the frame and then fading to black.

We left him drifting, rolling languorously in the dark water. Maybe he was dreaming of his war in the Pacific, of the cyber mines he'd swept, nosing gently into their circuitry with the Squid he'd used to pick Ralfi's pathetic password from the chip buried in my head.

"I can see them slipping up when he was demobbed, letting him out of the navy with that gear intact, but how does a cyber-netic dolphin get wired to smack?"

"The war," she said. "They all were. Navy did it. How else you get 'em working for you?"

"i'm not sure this profiles as good business," the pirate said, angling for better money. "Target specs on a comsat that isn't in the book—"

"Waste my time and you won't profile at all," said Molly, leaning across his scarred plastic desk to prod him with her forefinger.

"So maybe you want to buy your microwaves somewhere else?" He was a tough kid, behind his Mao-job. A Nighttowner by birth, probably.

Her hand blurred down the front of his jacket, completely severing a lapel without even rumpling the fabric.

"So we got a deal or not?"

"Deal," he said, staring at his ruined lapel with what he must have hoped was only polite interest. "Deal."

While I checked the two recorders we'd bought, she ex-tracted the slip of paper I'd given her from the zippered wrist pocket of her jacket. She unfolded it and read silently, moving her lips. She shrugged. "This is it?"

"Shoot," I said, punching the RECORD studs of the two decks simultaneously.

"Christian White," she recited, "and his Aryan Reggae Band."

Faithful Ralfi, a fan to his dying day.

Transition to idiot/savant mode is always less abrupt than I expect it to be. The pirate broadcaster's front was a failing travel agency in a pastel cube that boasted a desk, three chairs, and a faded poster of a Swiss orbital spa. A pair of toy birds with blown-glass bodies and tin legs were sipping monotonously from a Styrofoam cup of water on a ledge beside Molly's shoulder. As I phased into mode, they accelerated gradually until their Day-Glo-feathered crowns became solid arcs of color. The LEDs that told seconds on the plastic wall clock had become meaningless pulsing grids, and Molly and the Mao-faced boy grew hazy, their arms blurring occasionally in insect-quick ghosts of gesture. And then it all faded to cool gray static and an endless tone poem in an artificial language.

I sat and sang dead Ralfi's stolen program for three hours.

the mall runs forty kilometers from end to end, a ragged overlap of Fuller domes roofing what was once a suburban artery. If they turn off the arcs on a clear day, a gray approximation of sunlight filters through layers of acrylic, a view like the prison sketches of Giovanni Piranesi. The three southernmost kilometers roof Nighttown. Nighttown pays no taxes, no utilities. The neon arcs are dead, and the geodesics have been smoked black by decades of cooking fires. In the nearly total darkness of a Nighttown noon, who notices a few dozen mad children lost in the rafters?

We'd been climbing for two hours, up concrete stairs and

steel ladders with perforated rungs, past abandoned gantries and dust-covered tools. We'd started in what looked like a disused maintenance yard, stacked with triangular roofing segments. Everything there had been covered with that same uniform layer of spraybomb graffiti: gang names, initials, dates back to the turn of the century. The graffiti followed us up, gradually thinning until a single name was repeated at intervals. LO TEK. In dripping black capitals.

"Who's Lo Tek?"

"Not us, boss." She climbed a shivering aluminum ladder and vanished through a hole in a sheet of corrugated plastic. " 'Low technique, low technology.' " The plastic muffled her voice. I followed her up, nursing my aching wrist. "Lo Teks, they'd think that shotgun trick of yours was effete."

An hour later I dragged myself up through another hole, this one sawed crookedly in a sagging sheet of plywood, and met my first Lo Tek.

" 'S okay," Molly said, her hand brushing my shoulder. "It's just Dog. Hey, Dog."

In the narrow beam of her taped flash, he regarded us with his one eye and slowly extruded a thick length of grayish tongue, licking huge canines. I wondered how they wrote off tooth-bud transplants from Dobermans as low technology. Immunosuppressives don't exactly grow on trees.

"Moll." Dental augmentation impeded his speech. A string of saliva dangled from his twisted lower lip. "Heard ya comin'. Long time." He might have been fifteen, but the fangs and a bright mosaic of scars combined with the gaping socket to present a mask of total bestiality. It had taken time and a certain kind of creativity to assemble that face, and his posture told me he enjoyed living behind it. He wore a pair of decaying jeans, black with grime and shiny along the creases. His chest and feet were bare. He did something with his mouth that approximated a grin. "Bein' followed, you."

Far off, down in Nighttown, a water vendor cried his trade.

"Strings jumping, Dog?" She swung her flash to the side, and I saw thin cords tied to eyebolts, cords that ran to the edge and vanished.

"Kill the fuckin' light!"

She snapped it off.

"How come the one who's followin' you's got no light?"

"Doesn't need it. That one's bad news, Dog. Your sentries give him a tumble, they'll come home in easy-to-carry sections."

"This a *friend* friend, Moll?" He sounded uneasy. I heard his feet shift on the worn plywood.

"No. But he's mine. And this one," slapping my shoulder, "he's a friend. Got that?"

"Sure," he said, without much enthusiasm, padding to the platform's edge, where the eyebolts were. He began to pluck out some kind of message on the taut cords.

Nighttown spread beneath us like a toy village for rats; tiny windows showed candlelight, with only a few harsh, bright squares lit by battery lanterns and carbide lamps. I imagined the old men at their endless games of dominoes, under warm, fat drops of water that fell from wet wash hung out on poles between the plywood shanties. Then I tried to imagine him climbing patiently up through the darkness in his zoris and ugly tourist shirt, bland and unhurried. How was he tracking us?

"Good," said Molly. "He smells us."

"smoke?" dog dragged a crumpled pack from his pocket and prized out a flattened cigarette. I squinted at the trademark while he lit it for me with a kitchen match. Yiheyuan filters. Beijing Cigarette Factory. I decided that the Lo Teks were black marketeers. Dog and Molly went back to their argument, which seemed to revolve around Molly's desire to use some particular piece of Lo Tek real estate.

"I've done you a lot of favors, man. I want that floor. And I want the music."

"You're not Lo Tek. . . ."

This must have been going on for the better part of a twisted kilometer, Dog leading us along swaying catwalks and up rope ladders. The Lo Teks leech their webs and huddling places to the city's fabric with thick gobs of epoxy and sleep above the abyss in mesh hammocks. Their country is so attenuated that in places it consists of little more than holds for hands and feet, sawed into geodesic struts.

The Killing Floor, she called it. Scrambling after her, my new Eddie Bax shoes slipping on worn metal and damp plywood, I wondered how it could be any more lethal than the rest of the territory. At the same time I sensed that Dog's protests were ritual and that she already expected to get whatever it was she wanted.

Somewhere beneath us, Jones would be circling his tank, feeling the first twinges of junk sickness. The police would be boring the Drome regulars with questions about Ralfi. What did he do? Who was he with before he stepped outside? And the Yakuza would be settling its ghostly bulk over the city's data banks, probing for faint images of me reflected in numbered accounts, securities transactions, bills for utilities. We're an information economy. They teach you that in school. What they don't tell you is that it's impossible to move, to live, to operate at any level without leaving traces, bits, seemingly meaningless fragments of personal information. Fragments that can be retrieved, amplified . . .

But by now the pirate would have shuttled our message into line for blackbox transmission to the Yakuza comsat. A simple message: Call off the dogs or we wideband your program.

The program. I had no idea what it contained. I still don't. I only sing the song, with zero comprehension. It was probably research data, the Yakuza being given to advanced forms of industrial espionage. A genteel business, stealing from Ono-Sendai as a matter of course and politely holding their data for ransom, threatening to blunt the conglomerate's research edge by making the product public.

But why couldn't any number play? Wouldn't they be happier with something to sell back to Ono-Sendai, happier than they'd be with one dead Johnny from Memory Lane?

Their program was on its way to an address in Sydney, to a place that held letters for clients and didn't ask questions once you'd paid a small retainer. Fourth-class surface mail. I'd erased most of the other copy and recorded our message in the resulting gap, leaving just enough of the program to identify it as the real thing.

My wrist hurt. I wanted to stop, to lie down, to sleep. I knew that I'd lose my grip and fall soon, knew that the sharp black shoes I'd bought for my evening as Eddie Bax would lose their purchase and carry me down to Nighttown. But he rose in my mind like a cheap religious hologram, glowing, the enlarged chip on his Hawaiian shirt looming like a reconnaissance shot of some doomed urban nucleus.

So I followed Dog and Molly through Lo Tek heaven, jury-rigged and jerry-built from scraps that even Nighttown didn't want.

The Killing Floor was eight meters on a side. A giant had threaded steel cable back and forth through a junkyard and drawn it all taut. It creaked when it moved, and it moved constantly, swaying and bucking as the gathering Lo Teks arranged themselves on the shelf of plywood surrounding it. The wood was silver with age, polished with long use and deeply etched with initials, threats, declarations of passion. This was suspended from a separate set of cables, which lost themselves in darkness beyond the raw white glare of the two ancient floods suspended above the Floor.

A girl with teeth like Dog's hit the Floor on all fours. Her breasts were tattooed with indigo spirals. Then she was across the Floor, laughing, grappling with a boy who was drinking dark liquid from a liter flask.

Lo Tek fashion ran to scars and tattoos. And teeth. The electricity they were tapping to light the Killing Floor seemed to be an exception to their overall aesthetic, made in the name of . . . ritual, sport, art? I didn't know, but I could see that the Floor was something special. It had the look of having been assembled over generations.

I held the useless shotgun under my jacket. Its hardness and heft were comforting, even though I had no more shells. And it came to me that I had no idea at all of what was really happening, or of what was supposed to happen. And that was the nature of my game, because I'd spent most of my life as a blind receptacle to be filled with other people's knowledge and then drained, spouting synthetic languages I'd never understand. A very technical boy. Sure.

And then I noticed just how quiet the Lo Teks had become.

He was there, at the edge of the light, taking in the Killing Floor and the gallery of silent Lo Teks with a tourist's calm. And as our eyes met for the first time with mutual recognition, a memory clicked into place for me, of Paris, and the long Mercedes electrics gliding through the rain to Notre Dame; mobile greenhouses, Japanese faces behind the glass, and a hundred

Nikons rising in blind phototropism, flowers of steel and crystal. Behind his eyes, as they found me, those same shutters whirring.

I looked for Molly Millions, but she was gone.

The Lo Teks parted to let him step up onto the bench. He bowed, smiling, and stepped smoothly out of his sandals, leaving them side by side, perfectly aligned, and then he stepped down onto the Killing Floor. He came for me, across that shifting trampoline of scrap, as easily as any tourist padding across synthetic pile in any featureless hotel.

Molly hit the Floor, moving.

The Floor screamed.

It was miked and amplified, with pickups riding the four fat coil springs at the corners and contact mikes taped at random to rusting machine fragments. Somewhere the Lo Teks had an amp and a synthesizer, and now I made out the shapes of speakers overhead, above the cruel white floods.

A drumbeat began, electronic, like an amplified heart, steady as a metronome.

She'd removed her leather jacket and boots; her T-shirt was sleeveless, faint telltales of Chiba City circuitry traced along her thin arms. Her leather jeans gleamed under the floods. She began to dance.

She flexed her knees, white feet tensed on a flattened gas tank, and the Killing Floor began to heave in response. The sound it made was like a world ending, like the wires that hold heaven snapping and coiling across the sky.

He rode with it, for a few heartbeats, and then he moved, judging the movement of the Floor perfectly, like a man stepping from one flat stone to another in an ornamental garden.

He pulled the tip from his thumb with the grace of a man at ease with social gesture and flung it at her. Under the floods, the filament was a refracting thread of rainbow. She threw herself flat and rolled, jackknifing up as the molecule whipped past, steel claws snapping into the light in what must have been an automatic rictus of defense.

The drum pulse quickened, and she bounced with it, her dark hair wild around the blank silver lenses, her mouth thin, lips taut with concentration. The Killing Floor boomed and roared, and the Lo Teks were screaming their excitement.

He retracted the filament to a whirling meter-wide circle of ghostly polychrome and spun it in front of him, thumbless hand held level with his sternum. A shield.

And Molly seemed to let something go, something inside, and that was the real start of her mad-dog dance. She jumped, twisting, lunging sideways, landing with both feet on an alloy engine block wired directly to one of the coil springs. I cupped my hands over my ears and knelt in a vertigo of sound, thinking Floor and benches were on their way down, down to Nighttown, and I saw us tearing through the shanties, the wet wash, exploding on the tiles like rotten fruit. But the cables held, and the Killing Floor rose and fell like a crazy metal sea. And Molly danced on it.

And at the end, just before he made his final cast with the filament, I saw something in his face, an expression that didn't seem to belong there. It wasn't fear and it wasn't anger. I think it was disbelief, stunned incomprehension mingled with pure aesthetic revulsion at what he was seeing, hearing—at what was happening to him. He retracted the whirling filament, the ghost disk shrinking to the size of a dinner plate as he whipped his arm above his head and brought it down, the thumbtip curving out for Molly like a live thing.

The Floor carried her down, the molecule passing just above her head; the Floor whiplashed, lifting him into the path of the taut molecule. It should have passed harmlessly over his head and been withdrawn into its diamond-hard socket. It took his hand off just behind the wrist. There was a gap in the Floor in front of him, and he went through it like a diver, with a strange deliberate grace, a defeated kamikaze on his way down to Nighttown. Partly, I think, he took the dive to buy himself a few seconds of the dignity of silence. She'd killed him with culture shock.

The Lo Teks roared, but someone shut the amplifier off, and Molly rode the Killing Floor into silence, hanging on now, her face white and blank, until the pitching slowed and there was only a faint pinging of tortured metal and the grating of rust on rust.

We searched the Floor for the severed hand, but we never found it. All we found was a graceful curve in one piece of rusted steel, where the molecule went through. Its edge was bright as new chrome.

WE NEVER learned whether the Yakuza had accepted our terms, or even whether they got our message. As far as I know, their program is still waiting for Eddie Bax on a shelf in the back room of a gift shop on the third level of Sydney Central-5. Probably they sold the original back to Ono-Sendai months ago. But maybe they did get the pirate's broadcast, because nobody's come looking for me yet, and it's been nearly a year. If they do come, they'll have a long climb up through the dark, past Dog's sentries, and I don't look much like Eddie Bax these days. I let Molly take care of that, with a local anesthetic. And my new teeth have almost grown in.

I decided to stay up here. When I looked out across the Killing Floor, before he came, I saw how hollow I was. And I knew I was sick of being a bucket. So now I climb down and visit Jones, almost every night.

We're partners now, Jones and I, and Molly Millions, too. Molly handles our business in the Drome. Jones is still in Funland, but he has a bigger tank, with fresh seawater trucked in once a week. And he has his junk, when he needs it. He still talks to the kids with his frame of lights, but he talks to me on a new display unit in a shed that I rent there, a better unit than the one he used in the navy.

And we're all making good money, better money than I made before, because Jones's Squid can read the traces of anything that anyone ever stored in me, and he gives it to me on the display unit in languages I can understand. So we're learning a lot about all my former clients. And one day I'll have a surgeon dig all the silicon out of my amygdalae, and I'll live with my own memories and nobody else's, the way other people do. But not for a while.

In the meantime it's really okay up here, way up in the dark, smoking a Chinese filtertip and listening to the condensation that drips from the geodesics. Real quiet up here—unless a pair of Lo Teks decide to dance on the Killing Floor.

It's educational, too. With Jones to help me figure things out, I'm getting to be the most technical boy in town.

ercifully, the whole thing is starting to fade, to become an episode. When I do still catch the odd glimpse, it's peripheral; mere fragments of mad-doctor chrome, confining themselves to the corner of the eye. There was that flying-wing liner over San Francisco last week, but it was almost translucent. And the shark-fin roadsters have gotten scarcer, and freeways discreetly avoid unfolding themselves into the gleaming eightylane monsters I was forced to drive last month in my rented Toyota. And I know that none of it will follow me to New York; my vision is narrowing to a single wavelength of probability. I've worked hard for that. Television helped a lot.

I suppose it started in London, in that bogus Greek taverna in Battersea Park Road, with lunch on Cohen's corporate tab. Dead steam-table food and it took them thirty minutes to find an ice bucket for the retsina. Cohen works for Barris-Watford, who publish big, trendy "trade" paperbacks: illustrated histories of the neon sign, the pinball machine, the windup toys of Occupied Japan. I'd gone over to shoot a series of shoe ads; California girls with tanned legs and frisky Day-Glo jogging shoes had capered for me down the escalators of St. John's Wood and across the platforms of Tooting Bec. A lean and hungry young agency had decided that the mystery of London Transport would sell waffle-tread nylon runners. They decide; I shoot. And Cohen, whom I knew vaguely from the old days in New York, had invited me to lunch the day before I was due out of Heathrow. He brought along a very fashionably dressed young woman named Dialta Downes, who was virtually chinless and evidently a noted pop-art historian. In retrospect, I see her walking in beside Cohen under a floating neon sign that flashes **THIS WAY LIES MADNESS** in huge sans-serif capitals.

Cohen introduced us and explained that Dialta was the prime mover behind the latest Barris-Watford project, an illustrated history of what she called "American Streamlined Moderne." Cohen called it "raygun Gothic." Their working title was *The Airstream Futuropolis: The Tomorrow That Never Was*.

There's a British obsession with the more baroque elements of American pop culture, something like the weird cowboys-and-Indians fetish of the West Germans or the aberrant French hunger for old Jerry Lewis films. In Dialta Downes this manifested itself in a mania for a uniquely American form of architecture that most Americans are scarcely aware of. At first I wasn't sure what she was talking about, but gradually it began to dawn on me. I found myself remembering Sunday morning television in the Fifties.

Sometimes they'd run old eroded newsreels as filler on the local station. You'd sit there with a peanut butter sandwich and a glass of milk, and a static-ridden Hollywood baritone would tell you that there was A Flying Car in Your Future. And three Detroit engineers would putter around with this big old Nash with wings, and you'd see it rumbling furiously down some deserted Michigan runway. You never actually saw it take off, but it flew away to Dialta Downes's never-never land, true home of a generation of completely uninhibited technophiles. She was talking about those odds and ends of "futuristic" Thirties and Forties architecture you pass daily in American cities without noticing; the movie marquees ribbed to radiate some mysterious energy, the dime stores faced with fluted aluminum, the chrome-tube chairs gathering dust in the lobbies of transient hotels. She saw these things as segments of a dreamworld, abandoned in the uncaring present; she wanted me to photograph them for her.

The Thirties had seen the first generation of American industrial designers; until the Thirties, all pencil sharpeners had looked like pencil sharpeners—your basic Victorian mechanism, perhaps with a curlicue of decorative trim. After the advent of the designers, some pencil sharpeners looked as though they'd been put together in wind tunnels. For the most part, the change was only skin-deep; under the streamlined chrome shell, you'd find the same Victorian mechanism. Which made a certain kind of sense, because the most successful American designers had been recruited from the ranks of Broadway theater designers. It was all a stage set, a series of elaborate props for playing at living in the future.

Over coffee, Cohen produced a fat manila envelope full of glossies. I saw the winged statues that guard the Hoover Dam, forty-foot concrete hood ornaments leaning steadfastly into an imaginary hurricane. I saw a dozen shots of Frank Lloyd Wright's Johnson's Wax Building, juxtaposed with the covers of old *Amazing Stories* pulps, by an artist named Frank R. Paul; the employees of Johnson's Wax must have felt as though they were walking into one of Paul's spray-paint pulp utopias. Wright's building looked as though it had been designed for people who wore white togas and Lucite sandals. I hesitated over one sketch of a particularly grandiose prop-driven airliner, all wing, like a fat symmetrical boomerang with windows in unlikely places. Labeled arrows indicated the locations of the grand ballroom and two squash courts. It was dated 1936.

"This thing couldn't have flown . . . ?" I looked at Dialta Downes.

"Oh, no, quite impossible, even with those twelve giant props; but they loved the look, don't you see? New York to London in less than two days, first-class dining rooms, private cabins, sun decks, dancing to jazz in the evening . . . The designers were populists, you see; they were trying to give the public what it wanted. What the public wanted was the future."

i'd been in Burbank for three days, trying to suffuse a really dull-looking rocker with charisma, when I got the package from Cohen. It is possible to photograph what isn't there; it's damned hard to do, and consequently a very marketable talent. While I'm not bad at it, I'm not exactly the best, either, and this poor guy strained my Nikon's credibility. I got out, depressed because I do like to do a good job, but not totally depressed, because I did make sure I'd gotten the check for the job, and I decided to restore myself with the sublime artiness of the Barris-Watford assignment. Cohen had sent me some books on Thirties design, more photos of streamlined buildings, and a list of Dialta Downes's fifty favorite examples of the style in California.

Architectural photography can involve a lot of waiting; the building becomes a kind of sundial, while you wait for a shadow to crawl away from a detail you want, or for the mass and balance of the structure to reveal itself in a certain way. While I was waiting, I thought myself in Dialta Downes's America. When I isolated a few of the factory buildings on the ground glass of the Hasselblad, they came across with a kind of sinister totalitarian dignity, like the stadiums Albert Speer built for Hitler. But the rest of it was relentlessly tacky: ephemeral stuff extruded by the collective American subconscious of the Thirties, tending mostly to survive along depressing strips lined with dusty mo-

tels, mattress wholesalers, and small used-car lots. I went for
the gas stations in a big way.

During the high point of the Downes Age, they put Ming the
Merciless in charge of designing California gas stations. Favor-
ing the architecture of his native Mongo, he cruised up and
down the coast erecting raygun emplacements in white stucco.
Lots of them featured superfluous central towers ringed with
those strange radiator flanges that were a signature motif of the
style, and made them look as though they might generate potent
bursts of raw technological enthusiasm, if you could only find
the switch that turned them on. I shot one in San Jose an hour
before the bulldozers arrived and drove right through the struc-
tural truth of plaster and lathing and cheap concrete.

"Think of it," Dialta Downes had said, "as a kind of alternate
America: a 1980 that never happened. An architecture of broken dreams."

And that was my frame of mind as I made the stations of her
convoluted socioarchitectural cross in my red Toyota—as I
gradually tuned in to her image of a shadowy America-that-
wasn't, of Coca-Cola plants like beached submarines, and
fifth-run movie houses like the temples of some lost sect that
had worshiped blue mirrors and geometry. And as I moved
among these secret ruins, I found myself wondering what the
inhabitants of that lost future would think of the world I lived in.
The Thirties dreamed white marble and slip-stream chrome,
immortal crystal and burnished bronze, but the rockets on the
covers of the Gernsback pulps had fallen on London in the dead
of night, screaming. After the war, everyone had a car—no
wings for it—and the promised superhighway to drive it down,
so that the sky itself darkened, and the fumes ate the marble and
pitted the miracle crystal. . . .

And one day, on the outskirts of Bolinas, when I was setting up to shoot a particularly lavish example of Ming's martial architecture, I penetrated a fine membrane, a membrane of probability. . . .

Every so gently, I went over the Edge—

And looked up to see a twelve-engined thing like a bloated boomerang, all wing, thrumming its way east with an elephantine grace, so low that I could count the rivets in its dull silver skin, and hear—maybe—the echo of jazz.

i took it to Kihn.

Merv Kihn, free-lance journalist with an extensive line in Texas pterodactyls, redneck UFO contactees, bush-league Loch Ness monsters, and the Top Ten conspiracy theories in the loonier reaches of the American mass mind.

"It's good," said Kihn, polishing his yellow Polaroid shooting glasses on the hem of his Hawaiian shirt, "but it's not *mental*; lacks the true quill."

"But I saw it, Mervyn." We were seated poolside in brilliant Arizona sunlight. He was in Tucson waiting for a group of retired Las Vegas civil servants whose leader received messages from Them on her microwave oven. I'd driven all night and was feeling it.

"Of course you did. Of course you saw it. You've read my stuff; haven't you grasped my blanket solution to the UFO problem? It's simple, plain and country simple: people"—he settled the glasses carefully on his long hawk nose and fixed me with his best basilisk glare—"*see* . . . things. People see these things. Nothing's there, but people *see* them anyway. Because they need to, probably. You've read Jung, you should know the score. . . . In your case, it's so obvious: You admit you were thinking about this crackpot architecture, having fantasies. . . . Look, I'm sure

you've taken your share of drugs, right? How many people survived the Sixties in California without having the odd hallucina-
tion? All those nights when you discovered that whole armies of
Disney technicians had been employed to weave animated
holograms of Egyptian hieroglyphs into the fabric of your jeans,
say, or the times when—"

"But it wasn't like that."

"Of course not. It wasn't like that at all; it was 'in a setting of
clear reality,' right? Everything normal, and then there's the
monster, the mandala, the neon cigar. In your case, a giant Tom
Swift airplane. It happens *all the time*. You aren't even crazy. You
know that, don't you?" He fished a beer out of the battered
foam cooler beside his deck chair.

"Last week I was in Virginia. Grayson County. I interviewed
a sixteen-year-old girl who'd been assaulted by a *bar hade*."

"A what?"

"A bear head. The severed head of a bear. This *bar hade*, see,
was floating around on its own little flying saucer, looked kind of
like the hubcaps on cousin Wayne's vintage Caddy. Had red,
glowing eyes like two cigar stubs and telescoping chrome an-
tennas poking up behind its ears." He burped.

"It assaulted her? How?"

"You don't want to know; you're obviously impressionable.
'It was cold' "—he lapsed into his bad southern accent—" 'and
metallic.' It made electronic noises. Now that is the real thing,
the straight goods from the mass unconscious, friend; that little
girl is a witch. There's just no place for her to function in this
society. She'd have seen the devil, if she hadn't been brought up
on *The Bionic Man* and all those *Star Trek* reruns. She is clued into
the main vein. And she knows that it happened to her. I got out
ten minutes before the heavy UFO boys showed up with the
polygraph."

I must have looked pained, because he set his beer down carefully beside the cooler and sat up.

"If you want a classier explanation, I'd say you saw a semiotic ghost. All these contactee stories, for instance, are framed in a kind of sci-fi imagery that permeates our culture. I could buy aliens, but not aliens that look like Fifties' comic art. They're semiotic phantoms, bits of deep cultural imagery that have split off and taken on a life of their own, like the Jules Verne airships that those old Kansas farmers were always seeing. But you saw a different kind of ghost, that's all. That plane was part of the mass unconscious, once. You picked up on that, somehow. The important thing is not to worry about it."

I did worry about it, though.

Kihn combed his thinning blond hair and went off to hear what They had had to say over the radar range lately, and I drew the curtains in my room and lay down in air-conditioned darkness to worry about it. I was still worrying about it when I woke up. Kihn had left a note on my door; he was flying up north in a chartered plane to check out a cattle-mutilation rumor ("muties," he called them; another of his journalistic specialties).

I had a meal, showered, took a crumbling diet pill that had been kicking around in the bottom of my shaving kit for three years, and headed back to Los Angeles.

The speed limited my vision to the tunnel of the Toyota's headlights. The body could drive, I told myself, while the mind maintained. Maintained and stayed away from the weird peripheral window dressing of amphetamine and exhaustion, the spectral, luminous vegetation that grows out of the corners of the mind's eye along late-night highways. But the mind had its own ideas, and Kihn's opinion of what I was already thinking of as my "sighting" rattled endlessly, through my head in a tight, lopsided orbit. Semiotic ghosts. Fragments of the Mass Dream, whirling past in the wind of my passage. Somehow this feedback-loop aggravated the diet pill, and the speed-vegetation along the road began to assume the colors of infrared satellite images, glowing shreds blown apart in the Toyota's slipstream.

I pulled over, then, and a half-dozen aluminum beer cans winked goodnight as I killed the headlights. I wondered what time it was in London, and tried to imagine Dialta Downes having breakfast in her Hampstead flat, surrounded by streamlined chrome figurines and books on American culture.

Desert nights in that country are enormous; the moon is closer. I watched the moon for a long time and decided that Kihn was right. The main thing was not to worry. All across the continent, daily, people who were more normal than I'd ever aspired to be saw giant birds, Bigfeet, flying oil refineries; they kept Kihn busy and solvent. Why should I be upset by a glimpse of the 1930s pop imagination loose over Bolinas? I decided to go to sleep, with nothing worse to worry about than rattle-snakes and cannibal hippies, safe amid the friendly roadside garbage of my own familiar continuum. In the morning I'd drive down to Nogales and photograph the old brothels, something I'd intended to do for years. The diet pill had given up.

the light woke me, and then the voices.

The light came from somewhere behind me and threw shift-ing shadows inside the car. The voices were calm, indistinct, male and female, engaged in conversation.

My neck was stiff and my eyeballs felt gritty in their sockets. My leg had gone to sleep, pressed against the steering wheel. I fumbled for my glasses in the pocket of my work shirt and finally got them on.

Then I looked behind me and saw the city.

The books on Thirties' design were in the trunk; one of them contained sketches of an idealized city that drew on *Metropolis* and *Things to Come*, but squared everything, soaring up through an architect's perfect clouds to zeppelin docks and mad neon spires. That city was a scale model of the one that rose behind me. Spire stood on spire in gleaming ziggurat steps that climbed to a central golden temple tower ringed with the crazy radiator flanges of the Mongo gas stations. You could hide the Empire State Building in the smallest of those towers. Roads of crystal soared between the spires, crossed and recrossed by smooth silver shapes like beads of running mercury. The air was thick with ships: giant wing-liners, little darting silver things (sometimes one of the quicksilver shapes from the sky bridges rose gracefully into the air and flew up to join the dance), mile-long blimps, hovering dragonfly things that were gyrocopters . . .

I closed my eyes tight and swung around in the seat. When I opened them, I willed myself to see the mileage meter, the pale road dust on the black plastic dashboard, the overflowing ashtray.

"Amphetamine psychosis," I said. I opened my eyes. The dash was still there, the dust, the crushed filtertips. Very carefully, without moving my head, I turned the headlights on.

And saw them.

They were blond. They were standing beside their car, an aluminum avocado with a central shark-fin rudder jutting up from its spine and smooth black tires like a child's toy. He had his arm around her waist and was gesturing toward the city. They were both in white: loose clothing, bare legs, spotless white sun shoes. Neither of them seemed aware of the beams of my headlights. He was saying something wise and strong, and she was nodding, and suddenly I was frightened, frightened in an entirely different way. Sanity had ceased to be an issue; I knew, somehow, that the city behind me was Tucson—a dream Tucson thrown up out of the collective yearning of an era. That it was real, entirely real. But the couple in front of me lived in it, and they frightened me.

They were the children of Dialta Downes's '80-that-wasn't; they were Heirs to the Dream. They were white, blond, and they probably had blue eyes. They were American. Dialta had said that the Future had come to America first, but had finally passed it by. But not here, in the heart of the Dream. Here, we'd gone on and on, in a dream logic that knew nothing of pollution, the finite bounds of fossil fuel, or foreign wars it was possible to lose. They were smug, happy, and utterly content with themselves and their world. And in the Dream, it was *their* world.

Behind me, the illuminated city: Searchlights swept the sky for the sheer joy of it. I imagined them thronging the plazas of white marble, orderly and alert, their bright eyes shining with enthusiasm for their floodlit avenues and silver cars.

It had all the sinister fruitiness of Hitler Youth propaganda.

I put the car in gear and drove forward slowly, until the bumper was within three feet of them. They still hadn't seen me. I rolled the window down and listened to what the man was saying. His words were bright and hollow as the pitch in some Chamber of Commerce brochure, and I knew that he believed in them absolutely.

"John," I heard the woman say, "we've forgotten to take our food pills." She clicked two bright wafers from a thing on her belt and passed one to him. I backed onto the highway and headed for Los Angeles, wincing and shaking my head.

———

i phoned Kihn from a gas station. A new one, in bad Spanish Modern. He was back from his expedition and didn't seem to mind the call.

"Yeah, that is a weird one. Did you try to get any pictures? Not that they ever come out, but it adds an interesting *frisson* to your story, not having the pictures turn out. . . ."

But what should I do?

"Watch lots of television, particularly game shows and soaps. Go to porn movies. Ever see *Nazi Love Motel*? They've got it on cable, here. Really awful. Just what you need."

What was he talking about?

"Quit yelling and listen to me. I'm letting you in on a trade secret: Really bad media can exorcise your semiotic ghosts. If it keeps the saucer people off my back, it can keep these Art Deco futuroids off yours. Try it. What have you got to lose?"

Then he begged off, pleading an early-morning date with the Elect.

"The who?"

"These oldsters from Vegas; the ones with the microwaves."

I considered putting a collect call through to London, getting Cohen at Barris-Watford and telling him his photographer was checked out for a protracted season in the Twilight Zone. In the end, I let a machine mix me a really impossible cup of black coffee and climbed back into the Toyota for the haul to Los Angeles.

Los Angeles was a bad idea, and I spent two weeks there. It was prime Downes country; too much of the Dream there, and too many fragments of the Dream waiting to snare me. I nearly wrecked the car on a stretch of overpass near Disneyland, when the road fanned out like an origami trick and left me swerving through a dozen minilanes of whizzing chrome teardrops with shark fins. Even worse, Hollywood was full of people who

looked too much like the couple I'd seen in Arizona. I hired an
Italian director who was making ends meet doing darkroom
work and installing patio decks around swimming pools until his
ship came in; he made prints of all the negatives I'd accumu-
lated on the Downes job. I didn't want to look at the stuff myself. It didn't seem to bother Leonardo, though, and when he
was finished I checked the prints, riffling through them like a
deck of cards, sealed them up, and sent them air freight to London. Then I took a taxi to a theater that was showing *Nazi Love
Motel,* and kept my eyes shut all the way.

Cohen's congratulatory wire was forwarded to me in San
Francisco a week later. Dialta had loved the pictures. He ad-
mired the way I'd "really gotten into it," and looked forward to
working with me again. That afternoon I spotted a flying wing
over Castro Street, but there was something tenuous about it, as
though it were only half there. I rushed into the nearest news-
stand and gathered up as much as I could find on the petroleum
crisis and the nuclear energy hazard. I'd just decided to buy a
plane ticket for New York.

"Hell of a world we live in, huh?" The proprietor was a thin
black man with bad teeth and an obvious wig. I nodded, fishing
in my jeans for change, anxious to find a park bench where I
could submerge myself in hard evidence of the human near-
dystopia we live in. "But it could be worse, huh?"

"That's right," I said, "or even worse, it could be perfect."

He watched me as I headed down the street with my little
bundle of condensed catastrophe.

t hat summer Parker had trouble sleeping.

There were power droughts; sudden failures of the delta-inducer brought painfully abrupt returns to consciousness.

To avoid these, he used patch cords, miniature alligator clips, and black tape to wire the inducer to a battery-operated ASP deck. Power loss in the inducer would trigger the deck's playback circuit.

He bought an ASP cassette that began with the subject asleep on a quiet beach. It had been recorded by a young blonde yogi with 20-20 vision and an abnormally acute color sense. The boy had been flown to Barbados for the sole purpose of taking a nap and his morning's exercise on a brilliant stretch of private beach. The microfiche laminate in the cassette's transparent case explained that the yogi could will himself through alpha to delta without an inducer. Parker, who hadn't been able to sleep without an inducer for two years, wondered if this was possible.

He had been able to sit through the whole thing only once, though by now he knew every sensation of the first five subjective minutes. He thought the most interesting part of the sequence was a slight editing slip at the start of the elaborate breathing routine: a swift glance down the white beach that picked out the figure of a guard patrolling a chain-link fence, a black machine pistol slung over his arm.

While Parker slept, power drained from the city's grids.

The transition from delta to delta-ASP was a dark implosion into other flesh. Familiarity cushioned the shock. He felt the cool sand under his shoulders. The cuffs of his tattered jeans flapped against his bare ankles in the morning breeze. Soon the boy would wake fully and begin his Ardha-Matsyendra-something; with other hands Parker groped in darkness for the ASP deck.

three in the morning.

Making yourself a cup of coffee in the dark, using a flash-light when you pour the boiling water.

Morning's recorded dream, fading: through other eyes, dark plume of a Cuban freighter—fading with the horizon it navigates across the mind's gray screen.

Three in the morning.

Let yesterday arrange itself around you in flat schematic im-ages. What you said—what she said—watching her pack—dialing the cab. However you shuffle them they form the same printed circuit, hieroglyphs converging on a central component; you, standing in the rain, screaming at the cabby.

The rain was sour and acid, nearly the color of piss. The cabby called you an asshole; you still had to pay twice the fare. She had three pieces of luggage. In his respirator and goggles, the man looked like an ant. He pedaled away in the rain. She didn't look back.

The last you saw of her was a giant ant, giving you the finger.

parker saw his first ASP unit in a Texas shantytown called Judy's Jungle. It was a massive console cased in cheap plastic chrome. A ten-dollar bill fed into the slot bought you five minutes of free-fall gymnastics in a Swiss orbital spa, trampolining through twenty-meter perihelions with a sixteen-year-old *Vogue* model—heady stuff for the Jungle, where it was simpler to buy a gun than a hot bath.

He was in New York with forged papers a year later, when two leading firms had the first portable decks in major department stores in time for Christmas. The ASP porn theaters that had boomed briefly in California never recovered.

Holography went too, and the block-wide Fuller domes that had been the holo temples of Parker's childhood became multi-level supermarkets, or housed dusty amusement arcades where you still might find the old consoles, under faded neon pulsing APPARENT SENSORY PERCEPTION through a blue haze of cigarette smoke.

Now Parker is thirty and writes continuity for broadcast ASP, programming the eye movements of the industry's human cameras.

the brown-out continues.

In the bedroom, Parker prods the brushed-aluminum face of his Sendai Sleep-Master. Its pilot light flickers, then lapses into darkness. Coffee in hand, he crosses the carpet to the closet she emptied the day before. The flashlight's beam probes the bare shelves for evidence of love, finding a broken leather sandal strap, an ASP cassette, and a postcard. The postcard is a white light reflection hologram of a rose.

At the kitchen sink, he feeds the sandal strap to the disposal unit. Sluggish in the brown-out, it complains, but swallows and digests. Holding it carefully between thumb and forefinger, he lowers the hologram toward the hidden rotating jaws. The unit emits a thin scream as steel teeth slash laminated plastic and the rose is shredded into a thousand fragments.

Later he sits on the unmade bed, smoking. Her cassette is in the deck ready for playback. Some women's tapes disorient him, but he doubts this is the reason he now hesitates to start the machine.

Roughly a quarter of all ASP users are unable to comfortably assimilate the subjective body picture of the opposite sex. Over the years some broadcast ASP stars have become increasingly androgynous in an attempt to capture this segment of the audience.

But Angela's own tapes have never intimidated him before. (But what if she has recorded a lover?) No, that can't be it—it's simply that the cassette is an entirely unknown quantity.

when parker was fifteen, his parents indentured him to the American subsidiary of a Japanese plastics combine. At the time, he felt fortunate; the ratio of applicants to indentured trainees was enormous. For three years he lived with his cadre in a dormitory, singing the company hymns in formation each morning and usually managing to go over the compound fence at least once a month for girls or the holodrome.

The indenture would have terminated on his twentieth birthday, leaving him eligible for full employee status. A week before his nineteenth birthday, with two stolen credit cards and a change of clothes, he went over the fence for the last time. He arrived in California three days before the chaotic New Secessionist regime collapsed. In San Francisco, warring splinter groups hit and ran in the streets. One or another of four different "provisional" city governments had done such an efficient

job of stockpiling food that almost none was available at street
level.

Parker spent the last night of the revolution in a burned-out
Tucson suburb, making love to a thin teenager from New Jersey
who explained the finer points of her horoscope between bouts
of almost silent weeping that seemed to have nothing at all to do
with anything he did or said.

Years later he realized that he no longer had any idea of his
original motive in breaking his indenture.

the first three quarters of the cassette have been erased;
you punch yourself fast-forward through a static haze of wiped
tape, where taste and scent blur into a single channel. The audio
input is white sound—the no-sound of the first dark sea. . . .
(Prolonged input from wiped tape can induce hypnagogic hal-
lucination.)

parker crouched in the roadside New Mexico brush at
midnight, watching a tank burn on the highway. Flame lit the
broken white line he had followed from Tucson. The explosion
had been visible two miles away, a white sheet of heat lightning
that had turned the pale branches of a bare tree against the night
sky into a photographic negative of themselves: carbon
branches against magnesium sky.

Many of the refugees were armed.

Texas owed the shantytowns that steamed in the warm Gulf
rains to the uneasy neutrality she had maintained in the face of
the Coast's attempted secession.

The towns were built of plywood, cardboard, plastic sheets
that billowed in the wind, and the bodies of dead vehicles. They

had names like Jump City and Sugaree, and loosely defined governments and territories that shifted constantly in the covert winds of a black-market economy.

Federal and state troops sent in to sweep the outlaw towns seldom found anything. But after each search, a few men would fail to report back. Some had sold their weapons and burned their uniforms, and others had come too close to the contraband they had been sent to find.

After three months, Parker wanted out, but goods were the only safe passage through the army cordons. His chance came only by accident: Late one afternoon, skirting the pall of greasy cooking smoke that hung low over the Jungle, he stumbled and nearly fell on the body of a woman in a dry creek bed. Flies rose up in an angry cloud, then settled again, ignoring him. She had a leather jacket, and at night Parker was usually cold. He began to search the creek bed for a length of brushwood.

In the jacket's back, just below her left shoulder blade, was a round hole that would have admitted the shaft of a pencil. The jacket's lining had been red once, but now it was black, stiff and shining with dried blood. With the jacket swaying on the end of his stick, he went looking for water.

He never washed the jacket; in its left pocket he found nearly an ounce of cocaine, carefully wrapped in plastic and transparent surgical tape. The right pocket held fifteen ampules of Megacillin-D and a ten-inch horn-handled switchblade. The antibiotic was worth twice its weight in cocaine.

He drove the knife hilt-deep into a rotten stump passed over by the Jungle's wood-gatherers and hung the jacket there, the flies circling it as he walked away.

That night, in a bar with a corrugated iron roof, waiting for one of the "lawyers" who worked passages through the cordon, he tried his first ASP machine. It was huge, all chrome and neon, and the owner was very proud of it; he had helped hijack the truck himself.

If the chaos of the Nineties reflects a radical shift in the paradigms of visual literacy, the final shift away from the Lascaux Gutenberg tradition of a pre-holographic society, what should we expect from this newer technology, with its promise of discrete encoding and subsequent reconstruction of the full range of sensory perception?

—*Roebuck and Pierhal, Recent American History: A Systems View*

fast-forward through the humming no-time of wiped tape—

—into her body. European sunlight. Streets of a strange city. Athens. Greek-letter signs and the smell of dust . . .

—*and the smell of dust.*

Look through her eyes (thinking, this woman hasn't met you yet; you're hardly out of Texas) at the gray monument, horses there in stone, where pigeons whirl up and circle—

—and static takes love's body, wipes it clean and gray. Waves of white sound break along a beach that isn't there. And the tape ends.

the inducer's light is burning now.

Parker lies in darkness, recalling the thousand fragments of the hologram rose. A hologram has this quality: Recovered and illuminated, each fragment will reveal the whole image of the rose. Falling toward delta, he sees himself the rose, each of his scattered fragments revealing a whole he'll never know—stolen

credit cards—a burned-out suburb—planetary conjunctions of
a stranger—a tank burning on a highway—a flat packet of
drugs—a switchblade honed on concrete, thin as pain.

Thinking: We're each other's fragments, and was it always
this way? That instant of a European trip, deserted in the gray
sea of wiped tape—is she closer now, or more real, for his having been there?

She had helped him get his papers, found him his first job in
ASP. Was that their history? No, history was the black face of
the delta-inducer, the empty closet, and the unmade bed. History was his loathing for the perfect body he woke in if the juice
dropped, his fury at the pedal-cab driver, and her refusal to
look back through the contaminated rain.

But each fragment reveals the rose from a different angle, he
remembered, but delta swept over him before he could ask
himself what that might mean.

The Belonging Kind

by John Shirley and William Gibson

i t might have been in Club Justine, or Jimbo's, or Sad Jack's, or the Rafters; Coretti could never be sure where he'd first seen her. At any time, she might have been in any one of those bars. She swam through the submarine half-life of bottles and glassware and the slow swirl of cigarette smoke . . . she moved through her natural element, one bar after another.

Now, Coretti remembered their first meeting as if he saw it through the wrong end of a powerful telescope, small and clear and very far away.

He had noticed her first in the Backdoor Lounge. It was called the Backdoor because you entered through a narrow back alley. The alley's walls crawled with graffiti, its caged lights ticked with moths. Flakes from its white-painted bricks crunched underfoot. And then you pushed through into a dim space inhabited by a faintly confusing sense of the half-dozen other bars that had tried and failed in the same room under different managements. Coretti sometimes went there because he liked the weary smile of the black bartender, and because the few customers rarely tried to get chummy.

He wasn't very good at conversation with strangers, not at parties and not in bars.

He was fine at the community college where he lectured in introductory linguistics; he could talk with the head of his department about sequencing and options in conversational

openings. But he could never talk to strangers in bars or at parties. He didn't go to many parties. He went to a lot of bars.

Coretti didn't know how to dress. Clothing was a language
and Coretti a kind of sartorial stutterer, unable to make the kind
of basic coherent fashion statement that would put strangers at
their ease. His ex-wife told him he dressed like a Martian; that
he didn't look as though he belonged anywhere in the city. He
hadn't liked her saying that, because it was true.

He hadn't ever had a girl like the one who sat with her back
arched slightly in the undersea light that splashed along the bar
in the Backdoor. The same light was screwed into the lenses of
the bartender's glasses, wound into the necks of the rows of
bottles, splashed dully across the mirror. In that light her dress
was the green of young corn, like a husk half stripped away,
showing back and cleavage and lots of thigh through the slits up
the side. Her hair was coppery that night. And, that night, her
eyes were green.

He pushed resolutely between the empty chrome-and-
Formica tables until he reached the bar, where he ordered a
straight bourbon. He took off his duffle coat, and wound up
holding it on his lap when he sat down one stool away from her.
Great, he screamed to himself, she'll think you're hiding an
erection. And he was startled to realize that he had one to hide.
He studied himself in the mirror behind the bar, a thirtyish man
with thinning dark hair and a pale, narrow face on a long neck,
too long for the open collar of the nylon shirt printed with en-
gravings of 1910 automobiles in three vivid colors. He wore a tie
with broad maroon and black diagonals, too narrow, he supposed, for what he now saw as the grotesquely long points of his
collar. Or it was the wrong color. Something.

Beside him, in the dark clarity of the mirror, the green-eyed
woman looked like Irma La Douce. But looking closer, studying

her face, he shivered. A face like an animal's. A beautiful face, but simple, cunning, two-dimensional. When she senses you're looking at her, Coretti thought, she'll give you the smile, disdainful amusement—or whatever you'd expect.

Coretti blurted, "May I, um, buy you a drink?"

At moments like these, Coretti was possessed by an agonizingly stiff, schoolmasterish linguistic tic. *Um*. He winced. *Um*.

"You would, um, like to buy me a drink? Why, how kind of you," she said, astonishing him. "That would be very nice." Distantly, he noticed that her reply was as stilted and insecure as his own. She added, "A Tom Collins, on this occasion, would be lovely."

On this occasion? Lovely? Rattled, Coretti ordered two drinks and paid.

A big woman in jeans and an embroidered cowboy shirt bellied up to the bar beside him and asked the bartender for change. "Well, hey," she said. Then she strutted to the jukebox and punched for Conway and Loretta's "You're the Reason Our Kids Are Ugly." Coretti turned to the woman in green, and murmured haltingly:

"Do you enjoy country-and-western music?" *Do you enjoy* . . . ? He groaned secretly at his phrasing, and tried to smile.

"Yes indeed," she answered, the faintest twang edging her voice, "I sure do."

The cowgirl sat down beside him and asked her, winking, "This li'l terror here givin' you a hard time?"

And the animal-eyed lady in green replied, "Oh, hell no, honey, I got my eye on 'im." And laughed. Just the right amount of laugh. The part of Coretti that was dialectologist stirred uneasily; too perfect a shift in phrasing and inflection. An actress? A talented mimic? The word *mimetic* rose suddenly in his mind,

but he pushed it aside to study her reflection in the mirror; the
rows of bottles occluded her breasts like a gown of glass.

"The name's Coretti," he said, his verbal poltergeist shifting
abruptly to a totally unconvincing tough-guy mode, "Michael
Coretti."

"A pleasure," she said, too softly for the other woman to
hear, and again she had slipped into the lame parody of Emily
Post.

"Conway and Loretta," said the cowgirl, to no one in particular.

"Antoinette," said the woman in green, and inclined her
head. She finished her drink, pretended to glance at a watch,
said thank-you-for-the-drink too damn politely, and left.

Ten minutes later Coretti was following her down Third Avenue. He had never followed anyone in his life and it both
frightened and excited him. Forty feet seemed a discreet distance, but what should he do if she happened to glance over her
shoulder?

Third Avenue isn't a dark street, and it was there, in the light
of a streetlamp, like a stage light, that she began to change. The
street was deserted.

She was crossing the street. She stepped off the curb and it
began. It began with tints in her hair—at first he thought they
were reflections. But there was no neon there to cast the blobs
of color that appeared, color sliding and merging like oil slicks.
Then the colors bled away and in three seconds she was white-
blond. He was sure it was a trick of the light until her dress
began to writhe, twisting across her body like shrink-wrap
plastic. Part of it fell away entirely and lay in curling shreds on
the pavement, shed like the skin of some fabulous animal. When
Coretti passed, it was green foam, fizzing, dissolving, gone. He
looked back up at her and the dress was another dress, green

satin, shifting with reflections. Her shoes had changed too. Her shoulders were bare except for thin straps that crossed at the small of her back. Her hair had become short, spiky.

He found that he was leaning against a jeweler's plate-glass window, his breath coming ragged and harsh with the damp of the autumn evening. He heard the disco's heartbeat from two blocks away. As she neared it, her movements began subtly to take on a new rhythm—a shift in emphasis in the sway of her hips, in the way she put her heels down on the sidewalk. The doorman let her pass with a vague nod. He stopped Coretti and stared at his driver's license and frowned at his duffle coat. Coretti anxiously scanned the wash of lights at the top of a milky plastic stairway beyond the doorman. She had vanished there, into robotic flashing and redundant thunder.

Grudgingly the man let him pass, and he pounded up the stairs, his haste disturbing the lights beneath the translucent plastic steps.

Coretti had never been in a disco before; he found himself in an environment designed for complete satisfaction-in-distraction. He waded nervously through the motion and the fashions and the mechanical urban chants booming from the huge speakers. He sought her almost blindly on the pose-clotted dance floor, amid strobe lights.

And found her at the bar, drinking a tall, lurid cooler and listening to a young man who wore a loose shirt of pale silk and very tight black pants. She nodded at what Coretti took to be appropriate intervals. Coretti ordered by pointing at a bottle of bourbon. She drank five of the tall drinks and then followed the young man to the dance floor.

She moved in perfect accord with the music, striking a series of poses; she went through the entire prescribed sequence, gracefully but not artfully, fitting in perfectly. Always, always fitting in perfectly. Her companion danced mechanically, moving through the ritual with effort.

When the dance ended, she turned abruptly and dived into the thick of the crowd. The shifting throng closed about her like something molten.

Coretti plunged in after her, his eyes never leaving her—and he was the only one to follow her change. By the time she reached the stair, she was auburn-haired and wore a long blue dress. A white flower blossomed in her hair, behind her right ear; her hair was longer and straighter now. Her breasts had become slightly larger; and her hips a shade heavier. She took the stairs two at a time, and he was afraid for her then. All those drinks.

But the alcohol seemed to have had no effect on her at all.

Never taking his eyes from her, Coretti followed, his heartbeat outspeeding the disco-throb at his back, sure that at any moment she would turn, glare at him, call for help.

Two blocks down Third she turned in at Lothario's. There was something different in her step now. Lothario's was a quiet complex of rooms hung with ferns and Art Deco mirrors. There were fake Tiffany lamps hanging from the ceiling, alternating with wooden-bladed fans that rotated too slowly to stir the wisps of smoke drifting through the consciously mellow drone of conversation. After the disco, Lothario's was familiar and comforting. A jazz pianist in pinstriped shirt sleeves and loosely knotted tie competed softly with talk and laughter from a dozen tables.

She was at the bar; the stools were only half taken, but Coretti chose a wall table, in the shadow of a miniature palm, and ordered bourbon.

He drank the bourbon and ordered another. He couldn't feel the alcohol much tonight.

She sat beside a young man, yet another young man with the usual set of bland, regular features. He wore a yellow golf shirt and pressed jeans. Her hip was touching his, just a little. They didn't seem to be speaking, but Coretti felt they were somehow communing. They were leaning toward one another slightly, silent. Coretti felt odd. He went to the rest room and splashed his face with water. Coming back, he managed to pass within three feet of them. Their lips didn't move till he was within earshot.

They took turns murmuring realistic palaver:

" . . . saw his earlier films, but—"

"But he's rather self-indulgent, don't you think?"

"Sure, but in the sense that . . ."

And for the first time, Coretti knew what they were, what they must be. They were the kind you see in bars who seem to have grown there, who seem genuinely at home there. Not drunks, but human fixtures. Functions of the bar. The belonging kind.

Something in him yearned for a confrontation. He reached his table, but found himself unable to sit down. He turned, took a deep breath, and walked woodenly toward the bar. He wanted to tap her on her smooth shoulder and ask who she was, and exactly what she was, and point out the cold irony of the fact that it was he, Coretti, the Martian dresser, the eavesdropper, the outsider, the one whose clothes and conversation never fit, who had at last guessed their secret.

But his nerve broke and he merely took a seat beside her and ordered bourbon.

"But don't you think," she asked her companion, "that it's all relative?"

The two seats beyond her companion were quickly taken by a couple who were talking politics. Antoinette and Golf Shirt took up the political theme seamlessly, recycling, speaking just loudly enough to be overheard. Her face, as she spoke, was expressionless. A bird trilling on a limb.

She sat so easily on her stool, as if it were a nest. Golf Shirt paid for the drinks. He always had the exact change, unless he wanted to leave a tip. Coretti watched them work their way methodically through six cocktails each, like insects feeding on nectar. But their voices never grew louder, their cheeks didn't redden, and when at last they stood, they moved without a trace of drunkenness—a weakness, thought Coretti, a gap in their camouflage.

They paid him absolutely no attention while he followed them through three successive bars.

As they entered Waylon's, they metamorphosed so quickly that Coretti had trouble following the stages of the change. It was one of those places with toilet doors marked Pointers and Setters, and a little imitation pine plaque over the jars of beef jerky and pickled sausages: *We've got a deal with the bank. They don't serve beer and we don't cash checks.*

She was plump in Waylon's, and there were dark hollows under her eyes. There were coffee stains on her polyester pantsuit. Her companion wore jeans, a T-shirt, and a red baseball cap with a red-and-white Peterbilt patch. Coretti risked losing them when he spent a frantic minute in "Pointers," blinking in confusion at a hand-lettered cardboard sign that said, *We aim to please—You aim too, please.*

Third Avenue lost itself near the waterfront in a petrified snarl of brickwork. In the last block, bright vomit marked the pavement at intervals, and old men dozed in front of black-and-white TVs, sealed forever behind the fogged plate glass of faded hotels.

The bar they found there had no name. An ace of diamonds

was gradually flaking away on the unwashed window, and the bartender had a face like a closed fist. An FM transistor in ivory plastic keened easy-listening rock to the uneven ranks of deserted tables. They drank beer and shots. They were old now, two ciphers who drank and smoked in the light of bare bulbs, coughing over a pack of crumpled Camels she produced from the pocket of a dirty tan raincoat.

At 2:25 they were in the rooftop lounge of the new hotel complex that rose above the waterfront. She wore an evening dress and he wore a dark suit. They drank cognac and pretended to admire the city lights. They each had three cognacs while Coretti watched them over two ounces of Wild Turkey in a Waterford crystal highball glass.

They drank until last call. Coretti followed them into the elevator. They smiled politely but otherwise ignored him. There were two cabs in front of the hotel; they took one, Coretti the other.

"Follow that cab," said Coretti huskily, thrusting his last twenty at the aging hippie driver.

"Sure, man, sure. . . ." The driver dogged the other cab for six blocks, to another, more modest hotel. They got out and went in. Coretti slowly climbed out of his cab, breathing hard.

He ached with jealousy: for the personification of conformity, this woman who was not a woman, this human wallpaper. Coretti gazed at the hotel—and lost his nerve. He turned away.

He walked home. Sixteen blocks. At some point he realized that he wasn't drunk. Not drunk at all.

in the morning he phoned in to cancel his early class. But his hangover never quite came. His mouth wasn't desiccated, and staring at himself in the bathroom mirror he saw that his eyes weren't bloodshot.

In the afternoon he slept, and dreamed of sheep-faced people reflected in mirrors behind rows of bottles.

that night he went out to dinner, alone—and ate nothing. The food looked back at him, somehow. He stirred it about to make it look as if he'd eaten a little, paid, and went to a bar. And another. And another bar, looking for her. He was using his credit card now, though he was already badly in the hole under Visa. If he saw her, he didn't recognize her.

Sometimes he watched the hotel he'd seen her go into. He looked carefully at each of the couples who came and went. Not that he'd be able to spot her from her looks alone—but there should be a *feeling,* some kind of intuitive recognition. He watched the couples and he was never sure.

In the following weeks he systematically visited every boozy watering hole in the city. Armed at first with a city map and five torn Yellow Pages, he gradually progressed to the more obscure establishments, places with unlisted numbers. Some had no phone at all. He joined dubious private clubs, discovered unlicensed after-hours retreats where you brought your own, and sat nervously in dark rooms devoted to areas of fringe sexuality he had not known existed.

But he continued on what became his nightly circuit. He always began at the Backdoor. She was never there, or in the next place, or the next. The bartenders knew him and they liked to see him come in, because he brought drinks continuously, and never seemed to get drunk. So he stared at the other customers a bit—so what?

Coretti lost his job.

He'd missed classes too many times. He'd taken to watching the hotel when he could, even in the daytime. He'd been seen in too many bars. He never seemed to change his clothes. He re-fused night classes. He would let a lecture trail off in the middle as he turned to gaze vacantly out the window.

He was secretly pleased at being fired. They had looked at him oddly at faculty lunches when he couldn't eat his food. And now he had more time for the search.

Coretti found her at 2:15 on a Wednesday morning, in a gay bar called the Barn. Paneled in rough wood and hung with hal-ters and rusting farm equipment, the place was shrill with per-fume and laughter and beer. She was everyone's giggling sister, in a blue-sequined dress, a green feather in her coiffed brown hair. Through a sweeping sense of almost cellular relief, Coretti was aware of a kind of admiration, a strange pride he now felt in her—and her kind. Here, too, she belonged. She was a repre-sentative type, a fag-hag who posed no threat to the queens or their butchboys. Her companion had become an ageless man with carefully silvered temples, an angora sweater, and a trench coat.

They drank and drank, and went laughing—laughing just the right sort of laughter—out into the rain. A cab was waiting, its wipers duplicating the beat of Coretti's heart.

Jockeying clumsily across the wet sidewalk, Coretti scurried into the cab, dreading their reaction.

Coretti was in the back seat, beside her.

The man with silver temples spoke to the driver. The driver muttered into his hand mike, changed gears, and they flowed away into the rain and the darkened streets. The cityscape made no impression on Coretti, who, looking inwardly, was seeing the cab stop, the gray man and the laughing woman pushing him out and pointing, smiling, to the gate of a mental hospital. Or: the cab stopping, the couple turning, sadly shaking their heads. And a dozen times he seemed to see the cab stopping in an empty side street where they methodically throttled him. Coretti left dead in the rain. Because he was an outsider.

But they arrived at Coretti's hotel.

In the dim glow of the cab's dome light he watched closely as the man reached into his coat for the fare. Coretti could see the coat's lining clearly and it was one piece with the angora sweater. No wallet bulged there, and no pocket. But a kind of slit widened. It opened as the man's fingers poised over it, and it disgorged money. Three bills, folded, were extruded smoothly from the slit. The money was slightly damp. It dried, as the man unfolded it, like the wings of a moth just emerging from the chrysalis.

"Keep the change," said the belonging man, climbing out of the cab. Antoinette slid out and Coretti followed, his mind seeing only the slit. The slit wet, edged with red, like a gill.

The lobby was deserted and the desk clerk bent over a crossword. The couple drifted silently across the lobby and into the elevator, Coretti close behind. Once he tried to catch her eye, but she ignored him. And once, as the elevator rose seven floors above Coretti's own, she bent over and sniffed at the chrome wall ashtray, like a dog snuffling at the ground.

Hotels, late at night, are never still. The corridors are never entirely silent. There are countless barely audible sighs, the rustling of sheets, and muffled voices speaking fragments out of sleep. But in the ninth-floor corridor, Coretti seemed to move through a perfect vacuum, soundless, his shoes making no sound at all on the colorless carpet and even the beating of his outsider's heart sucked away into the vague pattern that decorated the wallpaper.

He tried to count the small plastic ovals screwed on the doors, each with its own three figures, but the corridor seemed to go on forever. At last the man halted before a door, a door veneered like all the rest with imitation rosewood, and put his hand over the lock, his palm flat against the metal. Something scraped softly and then the mechanism clicked and the door swung open. As the man withdrew his hand, Coretti saw a grayish-pink, key-shaped sliver of bone retract wetly into the pale flesh.

No light burned in that room, but the city's dim neon aura filtered in through venetian blinds and allowed him to see the faces of the dozen or more people who sat perched on the bed and the couch and the armchairs and the stools in the kitchenette. At first he thought that their eyes were open, but then he realized that the dull pupils were sealed beneath nictitating membranes, third eyelids that reflected the faint shades of neon from the window. They wore whatever the last bar had called for; shapeless Salvation Army overcoats sat beside bright suburban leisurewear, evening gowns beside dusty factory clothes, biker's leather by brushed Harris tweed. With sleep, all spurious humanity had vanished.

They were roosting.

His couple seated themselves on the edge of the Formica countertop in the kitchenette, and Coretti hesitated in the middle of the empty carpet. Light-years of that carpet seemed to separate him from the others, but something called to him across the distance, promising rest and peace and belonging. And still he hesitated, shaking with an indecision that seemed to rise from the genetic core of his body's every cell.

Until they opened their eyes, all of them simultaneously, the membranes sliding sideways to reveal the alien calm of dwellers in the ocean's darkest trench.

Coretti screamed, and ran away, and fled along corridors and down echoing concrete stairwells to cool rain and the nearly empty streets.

Coretti never returned to his room on the third floor of that hotel. A bored house detective collected the linguistics texts, the single suitcase of clothing, and they were eventually sold at auction. Coretti took a room in a boardinghouse run by a grim Baptist tee-totaler who led her roomers in prayer at the start of every over-cooked evening meal. She didn't mind that Coretti never joined them for those meals; he explained that he was given free meals at work. He lied freely and skillfully. He never drank at the boarding-house, and he never came home drunk. Mr. Coretti was a little odd, but always paid his rent on time. And he was very quiet.

Coretti stopped looking for her. He stopped going to bars. He drank out of a paper bag while going to and from his job at a publisher's warehouse, in an area whose industrial zoning per-mitted few bars.

He worked nights.

Sometimes, at dawn, perched on the edge of his unmade bed, drifting into sleep—he never slept lying down, now—he thought about her. Antoinette. And them. The belonging kind. Sometimes he speculated dreamily. . . . Perhaps they were like house mice, the sort of small animal evolved to live only in the walls of man-made structures.

A kind of animal that lives only on alcoholic beverages. With peculiar metabolisms they convert the alcohol and the various proteins from mixed drinks and wine and beers into everything they need. And they can change outwardly, like a chameleon or a rockfish, for protection. So they can live among us. And maybe, Coretti thought, they grow in stages. In the early stages seeming like humans, eating the food humans eat, sensing their difference only in a vague disquiet of being an outsider.

A kind of animal with its own cunning, its own special set of urban instincts. And the ability to know its own kind when they're near. Maybe.

And maybe not.

Coretti drifted into sleep.

On a Wednesday three weeks into his new job, his landlady opened the door—she never knocked—and told him that he was wanted on the phone. Her voice was tight with habitual suspicion, and Coretti followed her along the dark hallway to the second-floor sitting room and the telephone.

Lifting the old-fashioned black instrument to his ear, he heard only music at first, and then a wall of sound resolving into a fragmented amalgam of conversations. Laughter. No one spoke to him over the sound of the bar, but the song in the background was "You're the Reason Our Kids Are Ugly."

And then the dial tone, when the caller hung up.

later, alone in his room, listening to the landlady's firm tread in the room below, Coretti realized that there was no need to remain where he was. The summons had come. But the landlady demanded three weeks' notice if anyone wanted to leave. That meant that Coretti owed her money. Instinct told him to leave it for her.

A Christian workingman in the next room coughed in his sleep as Coretti got up and went down the hall to the telephone. Coretti told the evening-shift foreman that he was quitting his job. He hung up and went back to his room, locked the door behind him, and slowly removed his clothing until he stood naked before the garish framed lithograph of Jesus above the brown steel bureau.

And then he counted out nine tens. He placed them carefully beside the praying-hands plaque decorating the bureau top.

It was nice-looking money. It was perfectly good money. He made it himself.

this time, he didn't feel like making small talk. She'd been drinking a margarita, and he ordered the same. She paid, producing the money with a deft movement of her hand between the breasts bobbing in her low-cut dress. He glimpsed the gill closing there. An excitement rose in him—but somehow, this time, it didn't center in an erection.

After the third margarita their hips were touching, and something was spreading through him in slow orgasmic waves. It was sticky where they were touching; an area the size of the heel of his thumb where the cloth had parted. He was two men: the one inside fusing with her in total cellular communion, and the shell who sat casually on a stool at the bar, elbows on either side of his drink, fingers toying with a swizzle stick. Smiling benignly into space. Calm in the cool dimness.

And once, but only once, some distant worrisome part of him made Coretti glance down to where soft-ruby tubes pulsed, tendrils tipped with sharp lips worked in the shadows between them. Like the joining tentacles of two strange anemones.

They were mating, and no one knew.

And the bartender, when he brought the next drink, offered his tired smile and said, "Rainin' out now, innit? Just won't let up."

"Been like that all goddamn week," Coretti answered. "Rainin' to beat the band."

And he said it right. Like a real human being.

When Hiro hit the switch, I was dreaming of Paris, dreaming of wet, dark streets in winter. The pain came oscillating up from the floor of my skull, exploding behind my eyes in a wall of blue neon; I jackknifed up out of the mesh hammock, screaming. I always scream; I make a point of it. Feedback raged in my skull. The pain switch is an auxiliary circuit in the bonephone implant, patched directly into the pain centers, just the thing for cutting through a surrogate's barbiturate fog. It took a few seconds for my life to fall together, icebergs of biography looming through the fog: who I was, where I was, what I was doing there, who was waking me.

Hiro's voice came crackling into my head through the bone-conduction implant. "Damn, Toby. Know what it does to my ears, you scream like that?"

"Know how much I care about your *ears,* Dr. Nagashima? I care about them as much as—"

"No time for the litany of love, boy. We've got business. But what is it with these fifty-millivolt spike waves off your temporals, hey? Mixing something with the downers to give it a little color?"

"Your EEG's screwed, Hiro. You're crazy. I just want my sleep. . . ." I collapsed into the hammock and tried to pull the darkness over me, but his voice was still there.

"Sorry, my man, but you're working today. We got a ship back, an hour ago. Air-lock gang are out there right now, sawing the reaction engine off so she'll just about fit through the door."

"Who is it?"

"Leni Hofmannstahl, Toby, physical chemist, citizen of the Federal Republic of Germany." He waited until I quit groaning. "It's a confirmed meatshot."

Lovely workaday terminology we've developed out here. He meant a returning ship with active medical telemetry, contents one (1) body, warm, psychological status as yet unconfirmed. I shut my eyes and swung there in the dark.

"Looks like you're her surrogate, Toby. Her profile syncs with Taylor's, but he's on leave."

I knew all about Taylor's "leave." He was out in the agricultural canisters, ripped on amitriptyline, doing aerobic exercises to counter his latest bout with clinical depression. One of the occupational hazards of being a surrogate. Taylor and I don't get along. Funny how you usually don't, if the guy's psychosexual profile is too much like your own.

"Hey, Toby, where *are* you getting all that dope?" The question was ritual. "From Charmian?"

"From your mom, Hiro." He knows it's Charmian as well as I do.

"Thanks, Toby. Get up here to the Heavenside elevator in five minutes or I'll send those Russian nurses down to help you. The male ones."

I just swung there in my hammock and played the game called Toby Halpert's Place in the Universe. No egotist, I put the sun in the center, the luminary, the orb of day. Around it I swung tidy planets, our cozy home system. But just *here,* at a fixed point about an eighth of the way out toward the orbit of Mars, I hung a fat alloy cylinder, like a quarter-scale model of Tsiolkovsky 1, the Worker's Paradise back at L-5. Tsiolkovsky 1 is fixed at the liberation point between Earth's gravity and the moon's, but we need a lightsail to hold us here, twenty tons of aluminum spun into a hexagon, ten kilometers from side to side. That sail towed us out from Earth orbit, and now it's our anchor. We use it to tack against the photon stream, hanging here beside the thing— the point, the singularity—we call the Highway.

The French call it *le métro,* the subway, and the Russians call it the river, but *subway* won't carry the distance, and *river,* for Americans, can't carry quite the same loneliness. Call it the Tovyevski Anomaly Coordinates if you don't mind bringing Olga into it. Olga Tovyevski, Our Lady of Singularities, Patron Saint of the Highway.

Hiro didn't trust me to get up on my own. Just before the Russian orderlies came in, he turned the lights on in my cubicle, by remote control, and let them strobe and stutter for a few sec-onds before they fell as a steady glare across the pictures of Saint Olga that Charmian had taped up on the bulkhead. Dozens of them, her face repeated in newsprint, in magazine glossy. Our Lady of the Highway.

lieutenant colonel Olga Tovyevski, youngest woman of her rank in the Soviet space effort, was en route to Mars, solo, in a modified Alyut 6. The modifications allowed her to carry the prototype of a new airscrubber that was to be tested in the USSR's four-man Martian orbital lab. They could just as easily have handled the Alyut by remote, from Tsiolkovsky, but Olga wanted to log mission time. They made sure she kept busy, though; they stuck her with a series of routine hydrogen-band radio-flare experiments, the tail end of a low-priority Soviet-Australian scientific exchange. Olga knew that her role in the experiments could have been handled by a standard household timer. But she was a diligent officer; she'd press the buttons at precisely the correct intervals.

With her brown hair drawn back and caught in a net, she must have looked like some idealized *Pravda* cameo of the Worker in Space, easily the most photogenic cosmonaut of either gender. She checked the Alyut's chronometer again and poised her hand above the buttons that would trigger the first of her flares. Colonel Tovyevski had no way of knowing that she was nearing the point in space that would eventually be known as the Highway.

As she punched the six-button triggering sequence, the Alyut crossed those final kilometers and emitted the flare, a sustained burst of radio energy at 1420 mega-hertz, broadcast frequency of the hydrogen atom. Tsiolkovsky's radio telescope was tracking, relaying the signal to geosynchronous comsats that bounced it down to stations in the southern Urals and New South Wales. For 3.8 seconds the Alyut's radio image was obscured by the afterimage of the flare.

When the afterimage faded from Earth's monitor screens, the Alyut was gone.

In the Urals a middle-aged Georgian technician bit through the stem of his favorite meerschaum. In New South Wales a young physicist began to slam the side of his monitor, like an enraged pinball finalist protesting TILT.

the elevator that waited to take me up to Heaven looked like Hollywood's best shot at a Bauhaus mummy case—a narrow, upright sarcophagus with a clear acrylic lid. Behind it, rows of identical consoles receded like a textbook illustration of vanishing perspective. The usual crowd of technicians in yellow paper clown suits were milling purposefully around. I spotted

Hiro in blue denim, his pearl-buttoned cowboy shirt open over a faded UCLA sweat shirt. Engrossed in the figures cascading down the face of a monitor screen, he didn't notice me. Neither did anyone else.

So I just stood there and stared up at the ceiling, at the bottom of the floor of Heaven. It didn't look like much. Our fat cylinder is actually two cylinders, one inside the other. Down here in the outer one—we make our own "down" with axial rotation—are all the more mundane aspects of our operation: dormitories, cafeterias, the air-lock deck, where we haul in returning boats, Communications—and Wards, where I'm careful never to go.

Heaven, the inner cylinder, the unlikely green heart of this place, is the ripe Disney dream of homecoming, the ravenous ear of an information-hungry global economy. A constant stream of raw data goes pulsing home to Earth, a flood of rumors, whispers, hints of transgalactic traffic. I used to lie rigid in my hammock and feel the pressure of all those data, feel them snaking through the lines I imagined behind the bulkhead, lines like sinews, strapped and bulging, ready to spasm, ready to crush me. Then Charmian moved in with me, and after I told her about the fear, she made magic against it and put up her icons of Saint Olga. And the pressure receded, fell away.

"Patching you in with a translator, Toby. You may need German this morning." His voice was sand in my skull, a dry modulation of static. "Hillary—"

"On line, Dr. Nagashima," said a BBC voice, clear as ice crystal. "You do have French, do you, Toby? Hofmannstahl has French and English."

"You stay the hell out of my hair, Hillary. Speak when you're bloody spoken to, got it?" Her silence became another layer in the complex, continual sizzle of static. Hiro shot me a dirty look across two dozen consoles. I grinned.

It was starting to happen: the elation, the adrenaline rush. I could feel it through the last wisps of barbiturate. A kid with a surfer's smooth, blond face was helping me into a jump suit. It smelled; it was new-old, carefully battered, soaked with synthetic sweat and customized pheromones. Both sleeves were plastered from wrist to shoulder with embroidered patches, mostly corporate logos, subsidiary backers of an imaginary Highway expedition, with the main backer's much larger trademark stitched across my shoulders—the firm that was supposed to have sent HALPERT, TOBY out to his rendezvous with the stars. At least my name was real, embroidered in scarlet nylon capitals just above my heart.

The surfer boy had the kind of standard-issue good looks I associate with junior partners in the CIA, but his name tape said NEVSKY and repeated itself in Cyrillic. KGB, then. He was no *tsi-olnik;* he didn't have that loose-jointed style conferred by twenty years in the L-5 habitat. The kid was pure Moscow, a polite clipboard ticker who probably knew eight ways to kill with a rolled newspaper. Now we began the ritual of drugs and pockets; he tucked a microsyringe, loaded with one of the new euphorohallucinogens, into the pocket on my left wrist, took a step back, then ticked it off on his clipboard. The printed outline of a jump-suited surrogate on his special pad looked like a handgun target. He took a five-gram vial of opium from the case he wore chained to his waist and found the pocket for that. Tick. Fourteen pockets. The cocaine was last.

Hiro came over just as the Russian was finishing. "Maybe she has some hard data, Toby; she's a physical chemist, remember." It was strange to hear him acoustically, not as bone vibration from the implant.

"Everything's hard up there, Hiro."

"Don't I know it?" He was feeling it, too, that special buzz. We couldn't quite seem to make eye contact. Before the awkwardness could deepen, he turned and gave one of the yellow clowns the thumbs up.

Two of them helped me into the Bauhaus coffin and stepped back as the lid hissed down like a giant's faceplate. I began my ascent to Heaven and the homecoming of a stranger named Leni Hofmannstahl. A short trip, but it seems to take forever.

olga, who was our first hitchhiker, the first one to stick out her thumb on the wavelength of hydrogen, made it home in two years. At Tyuratam, in Kazakhstan, one gray winter morning, they recorded her return on eighteen centimeters of magnetic tape.

If a religious man—one with a background in film technology—had been watching the point in space where her Alyut had vanished two years before, it might have seemed to him that God had butt-spliced footage of empty space with footage of Olga's ship. She blipped back into our space-time like some amateur's atrocious special effect. A week later and they might never have reached her in time; Earth would have spun on its way and left her drifting toward the sun. Fifty-three hours after her return, a nervous volunteer named Kurtz, wearing an armored work suit, climbed through the Alyut's hatch. He was an East German specialist in space medicine, and American cigarettes were his secret vice; he wanted one very badly as he negotiated the air lock, wedged his way past a rectangular mass of airscrubber core, and chinned his helmet lights. The Alyut, even after two years, seemed to be full of breathable air. In the twin beams from the massive helmet, he saw tiny globules of blood and

vomit swinging slowly past, swirling in his wake, as he edged the
bulky suit out of the crawlway and entered the command module. Then he found her.

She was drifting above the navigational display, naked,
cramped in a rigid fetal knot. Her eyes were open, but fixed on
something Kurtz would never see. Her fists were bloody,
clenched like stone, and her brown hair, loose now, drifted
around her face like seaweed. Very slowly, very carefully, he
swung himself across the white keyboards of the command console and secured his suit to the navigational display. She'd gone
after the ship's communications gear with her bare hands, he
decided. He deactivated the work suit's right claw; it unfolded
automatically, like two pairs of vice-grip pliers pretending they
were a flower. He extended his hand, still sealed in a pressur-
ized gray surgical glove.

Then, as gently as he could, he pried open the fingers of her
left hand. Nothing.

But when he opened her right fist, something spun free and
tumbled in slow motion a few centimeters from the synthetic
quartz of his faceplate. It looked like a seashell.

Olga came home, but she never came back to life behind
those blue eyes. They tried, of course, but the more they tried,
the more tenuous she became, and, in their hunger to know, they
spread her thinner and thinner until she came, in her martyr-
dom, to fill whole libraries with frozen aisles of precious relics.
No saint was ever pared so fine; at the Plesetsk laboratories
alone, she was represented by more than two million tissue
slides, racked and numbered in the subbasement of a bomb-
proof biological complex.

They had better luck with the seashell. Exobiology suddenly
found itself standing on unnervingly solid ground: one and

seven-tenths grams of highly organized biological information, definitely extraterrestrial. Olga's seashell generated an entire subbranch of the science, devoted exclusively to the study of . . . Olga's seashell.

The initial findings on the shell made two things clear. It was the product of no known terrestrial biosphere, and as there were no other known biospheres in the solar system, it had come from another star. Olga had either visited the place of its origin or come into contact, however distantly, with something that was, or had once been, capable of making the trip.

They sent a Major Grosz out to the Tovyevski Coordinates in a specially fitted Alyut 9. Another ship followed him. He was on the last of his twenty hydrogen flares when his ship vanished. They recorded his departure and waited. Two hundred thirty-four days later he returned. In the meantime they had probed the area constantly, desperate for anything that might become the specific anomaly, the irritant around which a theory might grow. There was nothing: only Grosz's ship, tumbling out of control. He committed suicide before they could reach him, the Highway's second victim.

When they towed the Alyut back to Tsiolkovsky, they found that the elaborate recording gear was blank. All of it was in perfect working order; none of it had functioned. Grosz was flash-frozen and put on the first shuttle down to Plesetsk, where bulldozers were already excavating for a new subbasement.

Three years later, the morning after they lost their seventh cosmonaut, a telephone rang in Moscow. The caller introduced himself. He was the director of the Central Intelligence Agency of the United States of America. He was authorized, he said, to make a certain offer. Under certain very specific conditions, the Soviet Union might avail itself of the best minds in Western psychiatry. It was the understanding of his agency, he continued, that such help might currently be very welcome.

His Russian was excellent.

the bonephone static was a subliminal sandstorm. The elevator slid up into its narrow shaft through the floor of Heaven. I counted blue lights at two-meter intervals. After the fifth light, darkness and cessation.

Hidden in the hollow command console of the dummy Highway boat, I waited in the elevator like the secret behind the gimmicked bookcase in a children's mystery story. The boat was a prop, a set piece, like the Bavarian cottage glued to the plaster alp in some amusement park—a nice touch, but one that wasn't quite necessary. If the returnees accept us at all, they take us for granted; our cover stories and props don't seem to make much difference.

"All clear," Hiro said. "No customers hanging around." I reflexively massaged the scar behind my left ear, where they'd gone in to plant the bonephone. The side of the dummy console swung open and let in the gray dawn light of Heaven. The fake boat's interior was familiar and strange at the same time, like your own apartment when you haven't seen it for a week. One of those new Brazilian vines had snaked its way across the left viewport since my last time up, but that seemed to be the only change in the whole scene.

Big fights over those vines at the biotecture meetings, American ecologists screaming about possible nitrogen shortfalls. The Russians have been touchy about biodesign ever since they had to borrow Americans to help them with the biotic program back at Tsiolkovsky 1. Nasty problem with the rot eating the hydroponic wheat; all that superfine Soviet engineering and they still couldn't establish a functional ecosystem. Doesn't help that that initial debacle paved the way for us to be out here with them now. It irritates them; so they insist on the Brazilian vines, whatever— anything that gives them a chance to argue. But I like those vines: The leaves are heart-shaped, and if you rub one between your hands, it smells like cinnamon.

I stood at the port and watched the clearing take shape, as reflected sunlight entered Heaven. Heaven runs on Greenwich Standard; big Mylar mirrors were swiveling somewhere, out in bright vacuum, on schedule of a Greenwich Standard dawn. The recorded birdsongs began back in the trees. Birds have a very hard time in the absence of true gravity. We can't have real ones, because they go crazy trying to make do with centrifugal force.

The first time you see it, Heaven lives up to its name, lush and cool and bright, the long grass dappled with wildflowers. It helps if you don't know that most of the trees are artificial, or the amount of care required to maintain something like the op- timal balance between blue-green algae and diatom algae in the ponds. Charmian says she expects Bambi to come gamboling out of the woods, and Hiro claims he knows exactly how many Disney engineers were sworn to secrecy under the National Se- curity Act.

"We're getting fragments from Hofmannstahl," Hiro said. He might almost have been talking to himself; the handler- surrogate gestalt was going into effect, and soon we'd cease to be aware of each other. The adrenaline edge was tapering off. "Nothing very coherent. 'Schöne Maschine,' something . . . 'Beautiful machine' . . . Hillary thinks she sounds pretty calm, but right out of it."

"Don't tell me about it. No expectations, right? Let's go in loose." I opened the hatch and took a breath of Heaven's air; it was like cool white wine. "Where's Charmian?"

He sighed, a soft gust of static. "Charmian should be in Clearing Five, taking care of a Chilean who's three days home, but she's not, because she heard you were coming. So she's waiting for you by the carp pond. Stubborn bitch," he added.

charmian was flicking pebbles at the Chinese bighead carp. She had a cluster of white flowers tucked behind one ear, a wilted Marlboro behind the other. Her feet were bare and muddy, and she'd hacked the legs off her jump suit at midthigh. Her black hair was drawn back in a ponytail.

We'd met for the first time at a party out in one of the welding shops, drunken voices clanging in the hollow of the alloy sphere, homemade vodka in zero gravity. Someone had a bag of water for a chaser, squeezed out a double handful, and flipped it expertly into a rolling, floppy ball of surface tension. Old jokes about passing water. But I'm graceless in zero g. I put my hand through it when it came my way. Shook a thousand silvery little balls from my hair, batting at them, tumbling, and the woman beside me was laughing, turning slow somersaults, long, thin girl with black hair. She wore those baggy drawstring pants that tourists take home from Tsiolkovsky and a faded NASA T-shirt three sizes too big. A minute later she was telling me about hang-gliding with the teen *tsiolniki* and about how proud they'd been of the weak pot they grew in one of the corn canisters. I didn't realize she was another surrogate until Hiro clicked in to tell us the party was over. She moved in with me a week later.

"A minute, okay?" Hiro gritted his teeth, a horrible sound. "One. *Uno*." Then he was gone, off the circuit entirely, maybe not even listening.

"How's tricks in Clearing Five?" I squatted beside her and found some pebbles of my own.

"Not so hot. I had to get away from him for a while, shot him up with hypnotics. My translator told me you were on your way up." She has the kind of Texas accent that makes *ice* sound like *ass*.

"Thought you spoke Spanish. Guy's Chilean isn't he?" I tossed one of my pebbles into the pond.

"I speak Mexican. The culture vultures said he wouldn't like my accent. Good thing, too. I can't follow him when he talks fast." One of her pebbles followed mine, rings spreading on the surface as it sank. "Which is constantly," she added. A bighead swam over to see whether her pebble was good to eat. "He isn't going to make it." She wasn't looking at me. Her tone was perfectly neutral. "Little Jorge is definitely not making it."

I chose the flattest of my pebbles and tried to skip it across the pond, but it sank. The less I knew about Chilean Jorge, the better. I knew he was a live one, one of the ten percent. Our DOA count runs at twenty percent. Suicide. Seventy percent of the meatshots are automatic candidates for Wards: the diaper cases, mumblers, totally gone. Charmian and I are surrogates for that final ten percent.

If the first ones to come back had only returned with seashells, I doubt that Heaven would be out here. Heaven was built after a dead Frenchman returned with a twelve-centimeter ring of magnetically coded steel locked in his cold hand, black parody of the lucky kid who wins the free ride on the merry-go-round. We may never find out where or how he got it, but that ring was the Rosetta stone for cancer. So now it's cargo cult time for the human race. We can pick things up out there that we might not stumble across in research in a thousand years. Charmian says we're like those poor suckers on their island, who spend all their time building landing strips to make the big silver birds come back. Charmian says that contact with "superior" civilizations is something you don't wish on your worst enemy.

"Ever wonder how they thought this scam up, Toby?" She was squinting into the sunlight, east, down the length of our cylindrical country, horizonless and green. "They must've had all the heavies in, the shrink elite, scattered down a long slab of genuine imitation rosewood, standard Pentagon issue. Each one got a clean notepad and a brand-new pencil, specially sharpened for the occasion. Everybody was there: Freudians, Jungians, Adlerians, Skinner rat men, you name it. And every one of those bastards knew in his heart that it was time to play his best hand. As a profession, not just as representatives of a given faction. There they are, Western psychiatry incarnate. And nothing's happening! People are popping back off the Highway dead, or else they come back drooling, singing nursery rhymes. The live ones last about three days, won't say a goddamned thing, then shoot themselves or go catatonic." She took a small flashlight from her belt and casually cracked its plastic shell, extracting the parabolic reflector. "Kremlin's screaming. CIA's going nuts. And worst of all, the multinationals who want to back the show are getting cold feet. 'Dead spacemen? No data? No deal, friends.' So they're getting nervous, all those supershrinks, until some flake, some grinning weirdo from Berkeley maybe, he says," and her drawl sank to parody stoned mellowness, " 'Like, hey, why don't we just put these people into a real *nice* place with a lotta *good* dope and somebody they can really *relate* to, hey?' " She laughed, shook her head. She was using the reflector to light her cigarette, concentrating the sunlight. They don't give us matches; fires screw up the oxygen-carbon dioxide balance. A tiny curl of gray smoke twisted away from the white-hot focal point.

"Okay," Hiro said, "that's your minute." I checked my watch; it was more like three minutes.

"Good luck, baby," she said softly, pretending to be intent on her cigarette. "Godspeed."

the promise of pain. It's there each time. You know what will happen, but you don't know when, or exactly how. You try to hold on to them; you rock them in the dark. But if you brace for the pain, you can't function. That poem Hiro quotes, *Teach us to care and not to care.*

We're like intelligent houseflies wandering through an international airport; some of us actually manage to blunder onto flights to London or Rio, maybe even survive the trip and make it back. "Hey," say the other flies, "what's happening on the other side of that door? What do they know that we don't?" At the edge of the Highway every human language unravels in your hands—except, perhaps, the language of the shaman, of the cabalist, the language of the mystic intent on mapping hierarchies of demons, angels, saints.

But the Highway is governed by rules, and we've learned a few of them. That gives us something to cling to.

Rule One: One entity per ride; no teams, no couples.
Rule Two: No artificial intelligences; whatever's out there won't stop for a smart machine, at least, not the kind we know how to build.
Rule Three: Recording instruments are a waste of space; they always come back blank.

Dozens of new schools of physics have sprung up in Saint Olga's wake, ever more bizarre and more elegant heresies, each one hoping to shoulder its way to the inside track. One by one, they all fall down. In the whispering quiet of Heaven's nights, you imagine you can hear the paradigms shatter, shards of theory tinkling into brilliant dust as the lifework of some corporate think tank is reduced to the tersest historical footnote, and all in the time it takes your damaged traveler to mutter some fragment in the dark.

Flies in an airport, hitching rides. Flies are advised not to ask too many questions; flies are advised not to try for the Big Picture. Repeated attempts in that direction invariably lead to the slow, relentless flowering of paranoia, your mind projecting huge, dark patterns on the walls of night, patterns that have a way of solidifying, becoming madness, becoming religion. Smart flies stick with Black Box theory; Black Box is the sanctioned metaphor, the Highway remaining x in every sane equation. We aren't supposed to worry about what the Highway is, or who put it there. Instead, we concentrate on what we put into the Box and what we get back out of it. There are things we send down the Highway (a woman named Olga, her ship, so many more who've followed) and things that come to us (a madwoman, a seashell, artifacts, fragments of alien technologies). The Black Box theorists assure us that our primary concern is to optimize this exchange. We're out here to see that our species gets its money's worth. Still, certain things become increasingly evident; one of them is that we aren't the only flies who've found their way into an airport. We've collected artifacts from at least half a dozen wildly divergent cultures. "More hicks," Charmian calls them. We're like pack rats in the hold of a freighter, trading little pretties with rats from other ports. Dreaming of the bright lights, the big city.

Keep it simple, a matter of In and Out. Leni Hofmannstahl: Out.

———

WE STAGED the homecoming of Leni Hofmannstahl in Clearing Three, also known as Elysium. I crouched in a stand of meticulous reproductions of young vine maples and studied her ship. It had originally looked like a wingless dragonfly, a slender, ten-meter abdomen housing the reaction engine. Now, with the engine removed, it looked like a matte-white pupa, larval eye bulges stuffed with the traditional useless array of sensors and probes. It lay on a gentle rise in the center of the clearing, a specially designed hillock sculpted to support a variety of vessel formats. The newer boats are smaller, like Grand Prix washing machines, minimalist pods with no pretense to being exploratory vessels. Modules for meatshots.

"I don't like it," Hiro said. "I don't like this one. It doesn't feel right. . . ." He might have been talking to himself; he might almost have been *me* talking to myself, which meant the handler-surrogate gestalt was almost operational. Locked into my role, I'm no longer the point man for Heaven's hungry ear, a specialized probe radio-linked with an even more specialized psychiatrist; when the gestalt clicks, Hiro and I meld into something else, something we can never admit to each other, not when it isn't happening. Our relationship would give a classical Freudian nightmares. But I knew that he was right; something felt terribly wrong this time.

The clearing was roughly circular. It had to be; it was actually a fifteen-meter round cut through the floor of Heaven, a circular elevator disguised as an Alpine minimeadow. They'd sawed Leni's engine off, hauled her boat into the outer cylinder, lowered the clearing to the air-lock deck, then lifted her to Heaven on a giant pie plate landscaped with grass and wildflowers. They'd blanked her sensors with broadcast overrides and sealed her ports and hatch; Heaven is supposed to be a surprise to the newly arrived.

I found myself wondering whether Charmian was back with Jorge yet. Maybe she'd be cooking something for him, one of the fish we "catch" as they're released into our hands from cages on the pool bottoms. I imagined the smell of frying fish, closed my eyes, and imagined Charmian wading in the shallow water, bright drops beading on her thighs, long-legged girl in a fish-pond in Heaven.

"Move, Toby! In now!"

My skull rang with the volume; training and the gestalt reflex already had me halfway across the clearing. "Goddamn, god-damn, goddamn. . . ." Hiro's mantra, and I knew it had managed to go *all* wrong, then. Hillary the translator was a shrill under-tone, BBC ice cracking as she rattled something out at top speed, something about anatomical charts. Hiro must have used the remotes to unseal the hatch, but he didn't wait for it to un-screw itself. He triggered six explosive bolts built into the hull and blew the whole hatch mechanism out intact. It barely missed me. I had instinctively swerved out of its way. Then I was scrambling up the boat's smooth side, grabbing for the honey-comb struts just inside the entranceway; the hatch mechanism had taken the alloy ladder with it.

And I froze there, crouching in the smell of *plastique* from the bolts, because that was when the Fear found me, really found me, for the first time.

I'd felt it before, the Fear, but only the fringes, the least edge. Now it was vast, the very hollow of night, an emptiness cold and implacable. It was last words, deep space, every long goodbye in the history of our species. It made me cringe, whin-ing. I was shaking, groveling, crying. They lecture us on it, warn us, try to explain it away as a kind of temporary agoraphobia en-demic to our work. But we know what it is; surrogates know and handlers can't. No explanation has ever even come close.

It's the Fear. It's the long finger of Big Night, the darkness that feeds the muttering damned to the gentle white maw of Wards. Olga knew it first, Saint Olga. She tried to hide us from it, clawing at her radio gear, bloodying her hands to destroy her ship's broadcast capacity, praying Earth would lose her, let her die. . . .

Hiro was frantic, but he must have understood, and he knew what to do.

He hit me with the pain switch. Hard. Over and over, like a cattle prod. He drove me into the boat. He drove me through the Fear.

Beyond the Fear, there was a room. Silence, and a stranger's smell, a woman's.

The cramped module was worn, almost homelike, the tired plastic of the acceleration couch patched with peeling strips of silver tape. But it all seemed to mold itself around an absence. She wasn't there. Then I saw the insane frieze of ballpoint scratchings, crabbed symbols, thousands of tiny, crooked oblongs locking and overlapping. Thumb-smudged, pathetic, it covered most of the rear bulkhead.

Hiro was static, whispering, pleading. *Find her, Toby, now, please, Toby, find her, find her, find—*

I found her in the surgical bay, a narrow alcove off the crawlway. Above her, the *Schöne Maschine,* the surgical manipulator, glittering, its bright, thin arms neatly folded, chromed limbs of a spider crab, tipped with hemostats, forceps, laser scalpel. Hillary was hysterical, half-lost on some faint channel, something about the anatomy of the human arm, the tendons, the arteries, basic taxonomy. Hillary was screaming.

There was no blood at all. The manipulator is a clean machine, able to do a no-mess job in zero g, vacuuming the blood away. She'd died just before Hiro had blown the hatch, her right arm spread out across the white plastic work surface like a medieval drawing, flayed, muscles and other tissues tacked out in a neat symmetrical display, held with a dozen stainless-steel dissecting pins. She bled to death. A surgical manipulator is carefully programmed against suicides, but it can double as a robot dissector, preparing biologicals for storage.

She'd found a way to fool it. You usually can, with machines, given time. She'd had eight years.

She lay there in a collapsible framework, a thing like the fossil skeleton of a dentist's chair; through it, I could see the faded embroidery across the back of her jump suit, the trademark of a West German electronics conglomerate. I tried to tell her. I said, "Please, you're dead. Forgive us, we came to try to help, Hiro and I. Understand? He *knows* you, see, Hiro, he's here in my head. He's read your dossier, your sexual profile, your favorite colors; he knows your childhood fears, first lover, name of a teacher you liked. And I've got just the right pheromones, and I'm a walking arsenal of drugs, something here you're bound to like. And we can lie, Hiro and I; we're ace liars. Please. You've got to see. Perfect strangers, but Hiro and I, for you, we make up the *perfect* stranger, Leni."

She was a small woman, blond, her smooth, straight hair streaked with premature gray. I touched her hair, once, and went out into the clearing. As I stood there, the long grass shuddered, the wildflowers began to shake, and we began our descent, the boat centered on its landscaped round of elevator. The clearing slid down out of Heaven, and the sunlight was lost in the glare of huge vapor arcs that threw hard shadows across the broad deck of the air lock. Figures in red suits, running. A red Dinky Toy did a U-turn on fat rubber wheels, getting out of our way.

Nevsky, the KGB surfer, was waiting at the foot of the gangway that they wheeled to the edge of the clearing. I didn't see him until I reached the bottom.

"I must take the drugs now, Mr. Halpert."

I stood there, swaying, blinking tears from my eyes. He reached out to steady me. I wondered whether he even knew why he was down here in the lock deck, a yellow suit in red territory. But he probably didn't mind; he didn't seem to mind anything very much; he had his clipboard ready.

"I must take them, Mr. Halpert."

I stripped out of the suit, bundled it, and handed it to him. He stuffed it into a plastic Ziploc, put the Ziploc in a case manacled to his left wrist, and spun the combination.

"Don't take them all at once, kid," I said. Then I fainted.

late that night Charmian brought a special kind of darkness down to my cubicle, individual doses sealed in heavy foil. It was nothing like the darkness of Big Night, that sentient, hunting dark that waits to drag the hitchhikers down to Wards, that dark that incubates the Fear. It was a darkness like the shadows moving in the back seat of your parents' car, on a rainy night when you're five years old, warm and secure. Charmian's a lot slicker that I am when it comes to getting past the clipboard tickers, the ones like Nevsky.

I didn't ask her why she was back from Heaven, or what had happened to Jorge. She didn't ask me anything about Leni.

Hiro was gone, off the air entirely; I'd seen him at the debriefing that afternoon; as usual, our eyes didn't meet. It didn't matter. I knew he'd be back. It had been business as usual, really. A bad day in Heaven, but it's never easy. It's hard when you feel the Fear for the first time, but I've always known it was there, waiting. They talked about Leni's diagrams and about her ballpoint sketches of molecular chains that shift on command. Molecules that can function as switches, logic elements, even a kind of wiring, built up in layers into a single very large molecule, a very small computer. We'll probably never know what she met out there; we'll probably never know the details of the transaction. We might be sorry if we ever found out. We aren't the only hinterland tribe, the only ones looking for scraps.

Damn Leni, damn that Frenchman, damn all the ones who bring things home, who bring cancer cures, seashells, things without names—who keep us here waiting, who fill Wards, who bring us the Fear. But cling to this dark, warm and close, to Charmian's slow breathing, to the rhythm of the sea. You get high enough out here; you'll hear the sea, deep down behind the constant conch-shell static of the bonephone. It's something we carry with us, no matter how far from home.

Charmian stirred beside me, muttered a stranger's name, the name of some broken traveler long gone down to Wards. She holds the current record; she kept a man alive for two weeks, until he put his eyes out with his thumbs. She screamed all the way down, broke her nails on the elevator's plastic lid. Then they sedated her.

We both have the drive, though, that special need, that freak dynamic that lets us keep going back to Heaven. We both got it the same way, lay out there in our little boats for weeks, waiting for the Highway to take us. And when our last flare was gone, we were hauled back here by tugs. Some people just aren't taken, and nobody knows why. And you'll never get a second chance. They say it's too expensive, but what they really mean, as they eye the bandages on your wrists, is that now you're too valuable, too much use to them as a potential surrogate. Don't worry about the suicide attempt, they'll tell you; happens all the time. Perfectly understandable: feeling of profound rejection. But I'd wanted to go, wanted it so bad. Charmian, too. She tried with pills. But they worked on us, twisted us a little, aligned our drives, planted the bonephones, paired us with handlers.

Olga must have known, must have seen it all, somehow; she was trying to keep us from finding our way out there, where she'd been. She knew that if we found her, we'd have to go. Even now, knowing what I know, I still want to go. I never will. But we can swing here in this dark that towers way above us, Charmian's hand in mind. Between our palms the drug's torn foil wrapper. And Saint Olga smiles out at us from the walls; you can feel her, all those prints from the same publicity shot, torn and taped across the walls of night, her white smile, forever.

by Bruce Sterling and William Gibson

Colonel Korolev twisted slowly in his harness, dreaming of winter and gravity. Young again, a cadet, he whipped his horse across the late November steppes of Kazakhstan into dry red vistas of Martian sunset.

That's wrong, he thought—

And woke—in the Museum of the Soviet Triumph in Space—to the sounds of Romanenko and the KGB man's wife. They were going at it again behind the screen at the aft end of the Salyut, restraining straps and padded hull creaking and thudding rhythmically. Hooves in the snow.

Freeing himself from the harness, Korolev executed a practiced kick that propelled him into the toilet stall. Shrugging out of his threadbare coverall, he clamped the commode around his loins and wiped condensed steam from the steel mirror. His arthritic hand had swollen again during sleep; the wrist was bird-bone thin from calcium loss. Twenty years had passed since he'd last known gravity; he'd grown old in orbit.

He shaved with a suction razor. A patchwork of broken veins blotched his left cheek and temple, another legacy from the blowout that had crippled him.

When he emerged, he found that the adulterers had finished. Romanenko was adjusting his clothing. The political officer's wife, Valentina, had ripped the sleeves from her brown coverall; her white arms were sheened with the sweat of their exertion. Her ash-blond hair rippled in the breeze from a ventilator. Her eyes were purest cornflower blue, set a little too closely together, and they held a look half-apologetic, half-conspiratorial. "See what we've brought you, Colonel—"

She handed him a tiny airline bottle of cognac.

Stunned, Korolev blinked at the Air France logo embossed on the plastic cap.

"It came in the last Soyuz. In a cucumber, my husband said." She giggled. "He gave it to me."

"We decided you should have it, Colonel," Romanenko said, grinning broadly. "After all, we can be furloughed at any time." Korolev ignored the sidelong, embarrassed glance at his shriveled legs and pale, dangling feet.

He opened the bottle, and the rich aroma brought a sudden tingling rush of blood to his cheeks. He raised it carefully and sucked out a few milliliters of brandy. It burned like acid. "Christ," he gasped, "it's been years. I'll get plastered!" he said, laughing, tears blurring his vision.

"My father tells me you drank like a hero, Colonel, in the old days."

"Yes," Korolev said, and sipped again. "I did." The cognac spread through him like liquid gold. He disliked Romanenko. He'd never liked the boy's father, either—an easygoing Party man, long since settled into lecture tours, a dacha on the Black Sea, American liquor, French suits, Italian shoes. . . . The boy had the father's looks, the same clear gray eyes utterly untroubled by doubt.

The alcohol surged through Korolev's thin blood. "You are too generous," he said. He kicked once, gently, and arrived at his console. "You must take some *samisdata*, American cable broadcasts, freshly intercepted. Racy stuff! Wasted on an old man like me." He slotted a blank cassette and punched for the material.

"I'll give it to the gun crew," Romanenko said, grinning. "They can run it on the tracking consoles in the gun room." The particle-beam station had always been known as the gun room. The soldiers who manned it were particularly hungry for this sort of tape. Korolev ran off a second copy for Valentina.

"It's dirty?" She looked alarmed and intrigued. "May we come again, Colonel? Thursday at 2400?"

Korolev smiled at her. She had been a factory worker before she'd been singled out for space. Her beauty made her useful, as a propaganda tool, a role model for the proletariat. He pitied her now, with the cognac coursing through his veins, and found it impossible to deny her a little happiness. "A midnight rendezvous in the museum, Valentina? Romantic!"

She kissed his cheek, wobbling in free fall. "Thank you, my colonel."

"You're a prince, Colonel," Romanenko said, slapping Korolev's matchstick shoulder as gently as he could. After countless hours on an exerciser, the boy's arms bulged like a blacksmith's.

Korolev watched the lovers carefully make their way out into the central docking sphere, the junction of three aging Salyuts and two corridors. Romanenko took the "north" corridor to the gun room; Valentina went in the opposite direction to the next junction sphere and the Salyut where her husband slept.

There were five docking spheres in Kosmograd, each with its three linked Salyuts. At opposite ends of the complex were the military installation and the satellite launchers. Popping, humming, and wheezing, the station had the feel of a subway and the dank metallic reek of a tramp steamer.

Korolev had another pull at the bottle. Now it was half-empty. He hid it in one of the museum's exhibits, a NASA Hasselblad recovered from the site of the Apollo landing. He hadn't had a drink since his last furlough, before the blowout. His head swam in a pleasant, painful current of drunken nostalgia.

Drifting back to his console, he accessed a section of memory where the collected speeches of Alexei Kosygin had been covertly erased and replaced with his personal collection of *samisdata,* digitized pop music, his boyhood favorites from the Eighties. He had British groups taped from West German radio, Warsaw Pact heavy metal, American imports from the black market. Putting on his headphones, he punched for the Czestochowa reggae of Brygada Cryzis.

After all the years, he no longer really heard the music, but images came rushing back with an aching poignancy. In the Eighties he'd been a long-haired child of the Soviet elite, his father's position placing him effectively beyond the reach of the Moscow police. He remembered feedback howling through the speakers in the hot darkness of a cellar club, the crowd a shadowy checkerboard of denim and bleached hair. He'd smoked Marlboros laced with powdered Afghani hash. He remembered the mouth of an American diplomat's daughter in the back seat of her father's black Lincoln. Names and faces came flooding in on a warm haze of cognac. Nina, the East German who'd shown him her mimeographed translations of dissident Polish newssheets—

Until the night she didn't turn up at the coffee bar. Whispers of parasitism, of anti-Soviet activity, of the waiting chemical horrors of the *psikuska*—

Korolev started to tremble. He wiped his face and found it bathed in sweat. He took off the headphones.

It had been fifty years, yet he was suddenly and very intensely afraid. He couldn't remember ever having been this frightened, not even during the blowout that had crushed his hip. He shook violently. The lights. The lights in the Salyut were too bright, but he didn't want to go to the switches. A simple action, one he performed regularly, yet . . . The switches and their insulated cables were somehow threatening. He stared, confused. The little clockwork model of a Lunokhod moon rover, its Velcro wheels gripping the curved wall, seemed to crouch there like something sentient, poised, waiting. The eyes of the Soviet space pioneers in the official portraits were fixed on him with contempt.

The cognac. His years in free fall had warped his metabolism. He wasn't the man he'd once been. But he would remain calm and try to ride it out. If he threw up, everyone would laugh.

Someone knocked at the entrance to the museum, and Nikita the Plumber, Kosmograd's premier handyman, executed a perfect slow-motion dive through the open hatch. The young civilian engineer looked angry. Korolev felt cowed. "You're up early, Plumber," he said, anxious for some facade of normality.

"Pinhead leakage in Delta Three." He frowned. "Do you understand Japanese?" The Plumber tugged a cassette from one of the dozen pockets that bulged on his stained work vest and waved it in Korolev's face. He wore carefully laundered Levi's and dilapidated Adidas running shoes. "We accessed this last night."

Korolev cowered as though the cassette were a weapon. "No, no Japanese." The meekness of his own voice startled him. "Only English and Polish." He felt himself blush. The Plumber was his friend; he knew and trusted the Plumber, but—

"Are you well, Colonel?" The Plumber loaded the tape and punched up a lexicon program with deft, callused fingers. "You look as though you just ate a bug. I want you to hear this."

Korolev watched uneasily as the tape flickered into an ad for baseball gloves. The lexicon's Cyrillic subtitles raced across the monitor as a Japanese voice-over rattled maniacally.

"The newscast's coming up," said the Plumber, gnawing at a cuticle.

Korolev squinted anxiously as the translation slid across the face of the Japanese announcer:

AMERICAN DISARMAMENT GROUP CLAIMS . . . PREPARATIONS AT BAIKONUR COSMODROME . . . PROVE RUSSIANS AT LAST READY . . . TO SCRAP ARMED SPACE STATION COMIC CITY . . .

"Cosmic," the Plumber muttered. "Glitch in the lexicon."

BUILT AT TURN OF CENTURY AS BRIDGEHEAD TO SPACE . . . AMBITIOUS PROJECT CRIPPLED BY FAILURE OF LUNAR MINING . . . EXPENSIVE STATION OUTPERFORMED BY OUR UNMANNED ORBITAL FACTORIES . . . CRYSTALS, SEMICONDUCTORS AND PURE DRUGS . . .

"Smug bastards." The Plumber snorted. "I tell you, it's that goddamned KGB man Yefremov. He's had a hand in this!"

STAGGERING SOVIET TRADE DEFICITS . . . POPULAR DISCONTENT WITH SPACE EFFORT . . . RECENT DECISIONS BY POLITBURO AND CENTRAL COMMITTEE SECRETARIAT . . .

"They're shutting us down!" The Plumber's face contorted with rage.

Korolev twisted away from the screen, shaking uncontrollably. Sudden tears peeled from his lashes in free-fall droplets. "Leave me alone! I can do nothing!"

"What's wrong, Colonel?" The Plumber grabbed his shoulders. "Look me in the face. Someone's dosed you with the Fear!"

"Go away," Korolev begged.

"That little spook bastard! What has he given you? Pills? An injection?"

Korolev shuddered. "I had a drink—"

"He gave you the Fear! You, a sick old man! I'll break his

face!" The Plumber jerked his knees up, somersaulted back-ward, kicked off from a handhold overhead, and catapulted out of the room.

"Wait! Plumber!" But the Plumber had zipped through the docking sphere like a squirrel, vanishing down the corridor, and now Korolev felt that he couldn't bear to be alone. In the dis-tance he could hear metallic echoes of distorted, angry shouts.

Trembling, he closed his eyes and waited for someone to help him.

he'd asked Psychiatric Officer Bychkov to help him dress in his old uniform, the one with the Star of the Tsiolkovsky Order sewn above the left breast pocket. The black dress boots of heavy quilted nylon, with their Velcro soles, would no longer fit his twisted feet; so his feet remained bare.

Bychkov's injection had straightened him out within an hour, leaving him alternately depressed and furiously angry. Now, he waited in the museum for Yefremov to answer his sum-mons.

They called his home the Museum of the Soviet Triumph in Space, and as his rage subsided, to be replaced with an ancient bleakness, he felt very much as if he were simply another one of the exhibits. He stared gloomily at the gold-framed portraits of the great visionaries of space, at the faces of Tsiolkovsky, Rynin, Tupolev. Below these, in slightly smaller frames, were portraits of Verne, Goddard, and O'Neill.

In moments of extreme depression he had sometimes imag-ined that he could detect a common strangeness in their eyes, particularly in the eyes of the two Americans. Was it simply craziness, as he sometimes thought in his most cynical moods? Or was he able to glimpse a subtle manifestation of some weird, unbalanced force that he had often suspected of being human evolution in action?

Once, and only once, Korolev had seen that look in his own eyes—on the day he'd stepped onto the soil of the Coprates Basin. The Martian sunlight, glinting within his helmet visor, had shown him the reflection of two steady, alien eyes—fearless, yet driven—and the quiet, secret shock of it, he now realized, had been his life's most memorable, most transcendental moment.

Above the portraits, oily and inert, was a painting that depicted the landing in colors that reminded him of borscht and gravy, the Martian landscape reduced to the idealistic kitsch of Soviet Socialist realism. The artist had posed the suited figure beside the lander with all of the official style's deeply sincere vulgarity.

Feeling tainted, he awaited the arrival of Yefremov, the KGB man, Kosmograd's political officer.

When Yefremov finally entered the Salyut, Korolev noted the split lip and the fresh bruises on the man's throat. He wore a blue Kansai jump suit of Japanese silk and stylish Italian deck shoes. He coughed politely. "Good morning, Comrade Colonel."

Korolev stared. He allowed the silence to lengthen. "Yefremov," he said heavily, "I am not happy with you."

Yefremov reddened, but he held his gaze. "Let us speak frankly to each other, Colonel, as Russian to Russian. It was not, of course, intended for you."

"The Fear, Yefremov?"

"The beta-carboline, yes. If you hadn't pandered to their antisocial actions, if you hadn't accepted their bribe, it would not have happened."

"So I am a pimp, Yefremov? A pimp and a drunkard? You are

a cuckold, a smuggler, and an informer. I say this," he added, "as
one Russian to another."

Now the KGB man's face assumed the official mask of bland
and untroubled righteousness.

"But tell me, Yefremov, what it is that you are really about.
What have you been doing since you came to Kosmograd? We
know that the complex will be stripped. What is in store for the
civilian crew when they return to Baikonur? Corruption hear-
ings?"

"There will be interrogation, certainly. In certain cases
there may be hospitalization. Would you care to suggest,
Colonel Korolev, that the Soviet Union is somehow at fault for
Kosmograd's failures?"

Korolev was silent.

"Kosmograd was a dream, Colonel. A dream that failed. Like
space. We have no need to be here. We have an entire world to
put in order. Moscow is the greatest power in history. We must
not allow ourselves to lose the global perspective."

"Do you think we can be brushed aside that easily? We are
an elite, a highly trained technical elite."

"A minority, Colonel, an obsolete minority. What do you
contribute, aside from reams of poisonous American trash? The
crew here were intended to be workers, not bloated black marketeers trafficking in jazz and pornography." Yefremov's face
was smooth and calm. "The crew will return to Baikonur. The
weapons are capable of being directed from the ground. You, of
course, will remain, and there will be guest cosmonauts:
Africans, South Americans. Space still retains a degree of its
former prestige for these people."

Korolev gritted his teeth. "What have you done with the boy?"

"Your Plumber?" The political officer frowned. "He has assaulted an officer of the Committee for State Security. He will remain under guard until he can be taken to Baikonur."

Korolev attempted an unpleasant laugh. "Let him go. You'll be in too much trouble yourself to press charges. I'll speak with Marshal Gubarev personally. My rank may be entirely honorary, Yefremov, but I do retain a certain influence."

The KGB man shrugged. "The gun crew are under orders from Baikonur to keep the communications module under lock and key. Their careers depend on it."

"Martial law, then?"

"This isn't Kabul, Colonel. These are difficult times. You have the moral authority here; you should try to set an example."

"We shall see," Korolev said.

kosmograd swung out of Earth's shadow into raw sunlight. The walls of Korolev's Salyut popped and creaked like a nest of glass bottles. A Salyut's viewports, Korolev thought absently, fingering the broken veins at his temple, were always the first things to go.

Young Grishkin seemed to have the same thought. He drew a tube of caulk from an ankle pocket and began to inspect the seal around the viewport. He was the Plumber's assistant and closest friend.

"We must now vote," Korolev said wearily. Eleven of Kosmograd's twenty-four civilian crew members had agreed to attend the meeting, twelve if he counted himself. That left thirteen who were either unwilling to risk involvement or else actively hostile to the idea of a strike. Yefremov and the six-man gun crew brought the total number of those not present to twenty. "We've discussed our demands. All those in favor of the list as it stands—" He raised his good hand. Three others raised theirs. Grishkin, busy at the viewport stuck out his foot.

Korolev sighed. "There are few enough as it is. We'd best have unanimity. Let us hear your objections."

"The term *military custody*," said a biological technician named Korovkin, "might be construed as implying that the military, and not the criminal Yefremov, is responsible for the situation." The man looked acutely uncomfortable. "We are in sympathy otherwise but will not sign. We are Party members." He seemed about to add something but fell silent. "My mother," his wife said quietly, "was Jewish."

Korolev nodded, but he said nothing.

"This is all criminal foolishness," said Glushko, the botanist. Neither he nor his wife had voted. "Madness. Kosmograd is finished, we all know it, and the sooner home the better. What has this place ever been but a prison?" Free fall disagreed with the man's metabolism; in the absence of gravity, blood tended to congest in his face and neck, making him resemble one of his experimental pumpkins.

"You are a botanist, Vasili," his wife said stiffly, "while I, you will recall, am a Soyuz pilot. Your career is not at stake."

"I will *not* support this idiocy!" Glushko gave the bulkhead a savage kick that propelled him from the room. His wife followed, complaining bitterly in the grating undertone crew members learned to employ for private arguments.

"Five are willing to sign," Korolev said, "out of a civilian crew of twenty-four."

"Six," said Tatjana, the other Soyuz pilot, her dark hair drawn back and held with a braided band of green nylon webbing. "You forget the Plumber."

"The sun balloons!" cried Grishkin, pointing toward the earth. "Look!"

Kosmograd was above the coast of California now, clean shorelines, intensely green fields, vast decaying cities whose names rang with a strange magic. High above a fleece of stratocumulus floated live solar balloons, mirrored geodesic spheres tethered by power lines; they had been a cheaper substitute for a grandiose American plan to build solar-powered satellites. The things worked, Korolev supposed, because for the last decade he'd watched them multiply.

"And they say that people live in those things?" Systems Officer Stoiko had joined Grishkin at the viewport.

Korolev remembered the pathetic flurry of strange American energy schemes in the wake of the Treaty of Vienna. With the Soviet Union firmly in control of the world's oil flow, the Americans had seemed willing to try anything. Then the Kansas meltdown had permanently soured them on reactors. For more than three decades they'd been gradually sliding into isolationism and industrial decline. *Space,* he thought ruefully, *they should have gone into space.* He'd never understood the strange paralysis of will that had seemed to grip their brilliant early efforts. Or perhaps it was simply a failure of imagination, of vision. *You see, Americans,* he said silently, *you really should have tried to join us here in our glorious future, here in Kosmograd.*

"Who would want to live in something like that?" Stoiko asked, punching Grishkin's shoulder and laughing with the quiet energy of desperation.

"you're joking," said Yefremov. "Surely we're all in enough trouble as it is."

"We're not joking, Political Officer Yefremov, and these are our demands." The five dissidents had crowded into the Salyut the man shared with Valentina, backing him against the aft screen. The screen was decorated with a meticulously air-brushed photograph of the premier, who was waving from the back of a tractor. Valentina, Korolev knew, would be in the museum now with Romanenko, making the straps creak. The colonel wondered how Romanenko so regularly managed to avoid his duty shifts in the gun room.

Yefremov shrugged. He glanced down the list of demands. "The Plumber must remain in custody. I have direct orders. As for the rest of this document—"

"You are guilty of unauthorized use of psychiatric drugs!" Grishkin shouted.

"That was entirely a private matter," said Yefremov calmly.

"A criminal act," said Tatjana.

"Pilot Tatjana, we both know that Grishkin here is the station's most active *samisdata* pirate! We are all criminals, don't you see? That's the beauty of our system, isn't it?" His sudden, twisted smile was shockingly cynical. "Kosmograd is not the *Potemkin,* and you are not revolutionaries. And you *demand* to communicate with Marshal Gubarev? He is in custody at Baikonur. And you *demand* to communicate with the minister of technology? The minister is leading the purge." With a decisive gesture he ripped the printout to pieces, scraps of yellow flimsy scattering in free fall like slow-motion butterflies.

on the ninth day of the strike, Korolev met with Grishkin and Stoiko in the Salyut that Grishkin would ordinarily have shared with the Plumber.

For forty years the inhabitants of Kosmograd had fought an antiseptic war against mold and mildew. Dust, grease, and vapor wouldn't settle in free fall, and spores lurked everywhere—in padding, in clothing, in the ventilation ducts. In the warm, moist petri-dish atmosphere, they spread like oil slicks. Now there was a reek of dry rot in the air, overlaid with ominous whiffs of burning insulation.

Korolev's sleep had been broken by the hollow thud of a departing Soyuz lander. Glushko and his wife, he supposed. During the past forty-eight hours, Yefremov had supervised the evacuation of the crew members who had refused to join the strike. The gun crew kept to the gun room and their barracks ring, where they still held Nikita the Plumber.

Grishkin's Salyut had become strike headquarters. None of the male strikers had shaved, and Stoiko had contracted a staph infection that spread across his forearms in angry welts. Surrounded by lurid pinups from American television, they resembled some degenerate trio of pornographers. The lights were dim; Kosmograd ran on half-power. "With the others gone," Stoiko said, "our hand is strengthened."

Grishkin groaned. His nostrils were festooned with white streamers of surgical cotton. He was convinced that Yefremov would try to break the strike with beta-carboline aerosols. The cotton plugs were just one symptom of the general level of strain and paranoia. Before the evacuation order had come from Baikonur, one of the technicians had taken to playing Tchaikovsky's 1812 Overture at shattering volume for hours on end. And Glushko had chased his wife, naked, bruised, and screaming, up and down the length of Kosmograd. Stoiko had accessed the KGB man's files and Bychkov's psychiatric records; meters of yellow printout curled through the corridors in flabby spirals, rippling in the current from the ventilators.

"Think what their testimony will be doing to us groundside," muttered Grishkin. "We won't even get a trial. Straight to the *psikuska*." The sinister nickname for the political hospitals seemed to galvanize the boy with dread. Korolev picked apathetically at a viscous pudding of chlorella.

Stoiko snatched a drifting scroll of printout and read aloud. "Paranoia with a tendency to overesteem ideas! Revisionist fantasies hostile to the social system!" He crumpled the paper. "If we could seize the communications module, we could tie into an American comsat and dump the whole thing in their laps. Perhaps that would show Moscow something about our hostility!"

Korolev dug a stranded fruit fly from his algae pudding. Its two pairs of wings and bifurcated thorax were mute testimony to Kosmograd's high radiation levels. The insects had escaped from some forgotten experiment; generations of them had infested the station for decades. "The Americans have no interest in us," Korolev said. "Moscow can no longer be embarrassed by such revelations."

"Except when the grain shipments are due," Grishkin said.

"America needs to sell as badly as we need to buy." Korolev grimly spooned more chlorella into his mouth, chewed mechanically, and swallowed. "The Americans couldn't reach us even if they desired to. Canaveral is in ruins."

"We're low on fuel," Stoiko said.

"We can take it from the remaining landers," Korolev said.

"Then how in hell would we get back *down*?" Grishkin's fists trembled. "Even in Siberia, there are trees, trees; the sky! To hell with it! Let it fall to pieces! Let it fall and burn!"

Korolev's pudding spattered across the bulkhead.

"Oh, Christ," Grishkin said, "I'm sorry, Colonel. I know you can't go back."

———

when he entered the museum, he found Pilot Tatjana suspended before that hateful painting of the Mars landing, her cheeks slick with tears.

"Do you know, Colonel, they have a bust of you at Baikonur? In bronze. I used to pass it on my way to lectures." Her eyes were red-rimmed with sleeplessness.

"There are always busts. Academies need them." He smiled and took her hand.

"What was it like that day?" She still stared at the painting.

"I hardly remember. I've seen the tapes so often, now I remember them instead. My memories of Mars are any schoolchild's." He smiled for her again. "But it was not like this bad painting. In spite of everything, I'm still certain of that."

"Why has it all gone this way, Colonel? Why is it ending now? When I was small I saw all this on television. Our future in space was forever—"

"Perhaps the Americans were right. The Japanese sent machines instead, robots to build their orbital factories. Lunar mining failed for us, but we thought there would at least be a permanent research facility of some kind. It all had to do with purse strings, I suppose. With men who sit at desks and make decisions."

"Here is their final decision with regard to Kosmograd." She passed him a folded scrap of flimsy. "I found this in the printout of Yefremov's orders from Moscow. They'll allow the station's orbit to decay over the next three months."

He found that now he too was staring fixedly at the painting he loathed. "It hardly matters anymore," he heard himself say.

And then she was weeping bitterly, her face pressed hard against Korolev's crippled shoulder.

"But I have a plan, Tatjana," he said, stroking her hair. "You must listen."

he glanced at his old Rolex. They were over eastern Siberia. He remembered how the Swiss ambassador had presented him with the watch in an enormous vaulted room in the Grand Kremlin Palace.

It was time to begin.

He drifted out of his Salyut into the docking sphere, batting at a length of printout that tried to coil around his head.

He could still work quickly and efficiently with his good hand. He was smiling as he freed a large oxygen bottle from its webbing straps. Bracing himself against a handhold, he flung the bottle across the sphere with all his strength. It rebounded harmlessly with a harsh clang. He went after it, caught it, and hurled it again.

Then he hit the decompression alarm.

Dust spurted from speakers as a Klaxon began to wail. Triggered by the alarm, the docking bays slammed shut with a wheeze of hydraulics. Korolev's ears popped. He sneezed, then went after the bottle again.

The lights flared to maximum brilliance, then flickered out. He smiled in the darkness, groping for the steel bottle. Stoiko had provoked a general systems crash. It hadn't been difficult. The memory banks were already riddled to the point of collapse with bootlegged television broadcasts. "The real bare-knuckle stuff," he muttered, banging the bottle against the wall. The lights flickered on weakly as emergency cells came on line.

His shoulder began to ache. Stoically he continued pounding, remembering the din a real blowout caused. It had to be good. It had to fool Yefremov and the gun crew.

With a squeal, the manual wheel of one of the hatches began

to rotate. It thumped open, finally, and Tatjana looked in, grinning shyly.

"Is the Plumber free?" he asked, releasing the bottle.

"Stoiko and Umansky are reasoning with the guard." She drove a fist into her open palm. "Grishkin is preparing the landers."

He followed her up to the next docking sphere. Stoiko was helping the Plumber through the hatch that led from the barracks ring. The Plumber was barefoot, his face greenish under a scraggly growth of beard. Meteorologist Umansky followed them, dragging the limp body of a soldier.

"How are you, Plumber?" Korolev asked.

"Shaky. They've kept me on the Fear. Not big doses, but—and I thought that that was a real blowout!"

Grishkin slid out of the Soyuz lander nearest Korolev, trailing a bundle of tools and meters of a nylon lanyard. "They all check out. The crash left them under their own automatics. I've been at their remotes with a screwdriver so they can't be overridden by ground control. How are you doing, my Nikita?" he asked the Plumber. "You'll be going in steep to central China."

The Plumber winced, shook himself, and shivered. "I don't speak Chinese."

Stoiko handed him a printout. "This is in phonetic Mandarin. I WISH TO DEFECT. TAKE ME TO THE NEAREST JAPANESE EMBASSY."

The Plumber grinned and ran his fingers through his thatch of sweat-stiffened hair. "What about the rest of you?" he asked.

"You think we're doing this for your benefit alone?" Tatjana made a face at him. "Make sure the Chinese news services get the rest of that scroll, Plumber. Each of us has a copy. We'll see that the world knows what the Soviet Union intends to do to Colonel Yuri Vasilevich Korolev, first man on Mars!" She blew the Plumber a kiss.

"How about Filipchenko here?" Umansky asked. A few dark spheres of congealed blood swung crookedly past the unconscious soldier's cheek.

"Why don't you take the poor bastard with you," Korolev said.

"Come along then, shithead," the Plumber said, grabbing Filipchenko's belt and towing him toward the Soyuz hatch. "I, Nikita the Plumber, will do you the favor of your miserable lifetime."

Korolev watched as Stoiko and Grishkin sealed the hatch behind them.

"Where are Romanenko and Valentina?" Korolev asked, checking his watch again.

"Here, my colonel," Valentina said, her blond hair floating around her face in the hatch of another Soyuz. "We have been checking this one out." She giggled.

"Time enough for that in Tokyo," Korolev snapped. "They'll be scrambling jets in Vladivostok and Hanoi within minutes."

Romanenko's bare, brawny arm emerged and yanked her back into the lander. Stoiko and Grishkin sealed the hatch.

"Peasants in space." Tatjana made a spitting noise.

Kosmograd boomed hollowly as the Plumber, with the unconscious Filipchenko, cast off. Another boom and the lovers were off as well.

"Come along, friend Umansky," said Stoiko. "And farewell, Colonel!" The two men headed down the corridor.

"I'll go with you," Grishkin said to Tatjana. He grinned. "After all, you're a pilot."

"No," she said. "Alone. We'll split the odds. You'll be fine with the automatics. Just don't touch anything on the board."

Korolev watched her help him into the sphere's last Soyuz.

"I'll take you dancing, Tatjana," Grishkin said, "in Tokyo."

She sealed the hatch. Another boom, and Stoiko and Umansky had cast off from the next docking sphere.

"Go now, Tatjana," Korolev said. "Hurry. I don't want them shooting you down over international waters."

"That leaves you here alone, Colonel, alone with our enemies."

"When you've gone, they'll go as well," he said. "And I depend on your publicity to embarrass the Kremlin into keeping me alive here."

"And what shall I tell them in Tokyo, Colonel? Have you a message for the world?"

"Tell them . . ." and every cliché came rushing to him with an absolute rightness that made him want to laugh hysterically: *One small step . . . We came in peace . . . Workers of the world. . . .* "You must tell them that I need it," he said, pinching his shrunken wrist, "in my very bones."

She embraced him and slipped away.

he waited alone in the docking sphere. The silence scratched away at his nerves; the systems crash had deactivated the ventilation system, whose hum he'd lived with for twenty years. At last he heard Tatjana's Soyuz disengage.

Someone was coming down the corridor. It was Yefremov, moving clumsily in a vacuum suit. Korolev smiled.

Yefremov wore his bland, official mask behind the Lexan faceplate, but he avoided meeting Korolev's eyes as he passed. He was heading for the gun room.

"No!" Korolev shouted.

The Klaxon blared the station's call to full battle alert.

The gun-room hatch was open when he reached it. Inside, the soldiers were moving jerkily in the galvanized reflex of constant drill, yanking the broad straps of their console seats across the chests of their bulky suits.

"Don't do it!" He clawed at the stiff accordion fabric of Yefremov's suit. One of the accelerators powered up with a staccato whine. On a tracking screen, green cross hairs closed in on a red dot.

Yefremov removed his helmet. Calmly, with no change in his expression, he backhanded Korolev with the helmet.

"Make them stop!" Korolev sobbed. The walls shook as a beam cut loose with the sound of a cracking whip. "Your wife, Yefremov! She's out there!"

"Outside, Colonel." Yefremov grabbed Korolev's arthritic hand and squeezed. Korolev screamed. "Outside." A gloved fist struck him in the chest.

Korolev pounded helplessly on the vacuum suit as he was shoved out into the corridor. "Even I, Colonel, dare not come between the Red Army and its orders." Yefremov looked sick now; the mask had crumbled. "Fine sport," he said. "Wait here until it's over."

Then Tatjana's Soyuz struck the beam installation and the barracks ring. In a split-second daguerreotype of raw sunlight, Korolev saw the gun room wrinkle and collapse like a beer can crushed under a boot; he saw the decapitated torso of a soldier spinning away from a console; he saw Yefremov try to speak, his hair streaming upright as vacuum tore the air in his suit out through his open helmet ring. Fine twin streams of blood arced from Korolev's nostrils, the roar of escaping air replaced by a deeper roaring in his head.

The last thing Korolev remembered hearing was the hatch door slamming shut.

When he woke, he woke to darkness, to pulsing agony be-hind his eyes, remembering old lectures. This was as great a danger as the blowout itself, nitrogen bubbling through the blood to strike with white-hot, crippling pain. . . .

But it was all so remote, so academic, really. He turned the wheels of the hatches out of some strange sense of noblesse oblige, nothing more. The labor was quite onerous, and he wished very much to return to the museum and sleep.

he could repair the leaks with caulk, but the systems crash was beyond him. He had Glushko's garden. With the vegetables and algae, he wouldn't starve or smother. The communications module had gone with the gun room and the barracks ring, sheared from the station by the impact of Tatjana's suicidal Soyuz. He assumed that the collision had perturbed Kosmograd's orbit, but he had no way of predicting the hour of the station's final incandescent meeting with the upper atmosphere. He was often ill now, and he often thought that he might die before burnout, which disturbed him.

He spent uncounted hours screening the museum's library of tapes. A fitting pursuit for the Last Man in Space who had once been the First Man on Mars.

He became obsessed with the icon of Gagarin, endlessly re-running the grainy television images of the Sixties, the news-reels that led so unalterably to the cosmonaut's death. The stale air of Kosmograd swam with the spirits of martyrs. Gagarin, the first Salyut crew, the Americans roasted alive in their squat Apollo . . .

Often he dreamed of Tatjana, the look in her eyes like the look he'd imagined in the eyes of the museum's portraits. And once he woke, or dreamed he woke, in the Salyut where she had slept, to find himself in his old uniform, with a battery-powered work light strapped across his forehead. From a great distance, as though he watched a newsreel on the museum's monitor, he saw himself rip the Star of the Tsiolkovsky Order from his pocket and staple it to her pilot's certificate.

When the knocking came, he knew that it must be a dream as well.

The hatch wheeled open.

In the bluish, flickering light from the old film, he saw that the woman was black. Long corkscrews of matted hair rose like cobras around her head. She wore goggles, a silk aviator's scarf twisting behind her in free fall. "Andy," she said in English, "you better come see this!"

A small, muscular man, nearly bald, and wearing only a jockstrap and a jangling toolbelt floated up behind her and peered in. "Is he alive?"

"Of course I am alive," said Korolev in slightly accented English.

The man called Andy sailed in over her head. "You okay, Jack?" His right bicep was tattooed with a geodesic balloon above crossed lightning bolts and bore the legend SUNSPARK 15, UTAH. "We weren't expecting anybody."

"Neither was I," said Korolev, blinking.

"We've come to live here," said the woman, drifting closer.

"We're from the balloons. Squatters, I guess you could say. Heard the place was empty. You know the orbit's decaying on this thing?" The man executed a clumsy midair somersault, the tools clattering on his belt. "This free fall's outrageous."

"God," said the woman, "I just can't get used to it! It's wonderful. It's like skydiving, but there's no wind."

Korolev stared at the man, who had the blundering, careless look of someone drunk on freedom since birth. "But you don't even have a launchpad," he said.

"Launchpad?" the man said, laughing. "What we do, we

haul these surplus booster engines up the cables to the balloons, drop 'em, and fire 'em in midair."

"That's insane," Korolev said.

"Got us here, didn't it?"

Korolev nodded. If this was all a dream, it was a very peculiar one. "I am Colonel Yuri Vasilevich Korolev."

"Mars!" The woman clapped her hands. "Wait'll the kids hear that." She plucked the little Lunokhod moon-rover model from the bulkhead and began to wind it.

"Hey," the man said, "I gotta work. We got a bunch of boosters outside. We gotta lift this thing before it starts burning."

Something clanged against the hull. Kosmograd rang with the impact. "That'll be Tulsa," Andy said, consulting a wristwatch. "Right on time."

"But why?" Korolev shook his head, deeply confused. "Why have you come?"

"We told you. To live here. We can enlarge this thing, maybe build more. They said we'd never make it living in the balloons, but we were the only ones who could make them work. It was our one chance to get out here on our own. Who'd want to live out here for the sake of some government, some army brass, a bunch of pen pushers? You have to *want* a frontier—want it in your bones, right?"

Korolev smiled. Andy grinned back. "We grabbed those power cables and just pulled ourselves straight up. And when you get to the top, well, man, you either make that big jump or else you rot there." His voice rose. "And you don't look back, no sir! We've made that jump, and we're here to stay!"

The woman placed the model's Velcro wheels against the curved wall and released it. It went scooting along above their heads, whirring merrily. "Isn't that cute? The kids are just going to love it."

Korolev stared into Andy's eyes. Kosmograd rang again, jarring the little Lunokhod model onto a new course.

"East Los Angeles," the woman said. "That's the one with the kids in it." She took off her goggles, and Korolev saw her eyes brimming over with a wonderful lunacy.

"Well," said Andy, rattling his toolbelt, "you feel like showing us around?"

Seven rented nights in this coffin, Sandii. New Rose Hotel. How I want you now. Sometimes I hit you. Replay it so slow and sweet and mean, I can almost feel it. Sometimes I take your little automatic out of my bag, run my thumb down smooth, cheap chrome. Chinese .22, its bore no wider than the dilated pupils of your vanished eyes.

Fox is dead now, Sandii.

Fox told me to forget you.

i remember Fox leaning against the padded bar in the dark lounge of some Singapore hotel, Bencoolen Street, his hands describing different spheres of influence, internal rivalries, the arc of a particular career, a point of weakness he had discovered in the armor of some think tank. Fox was point man in the skull wars, a middleman for corporate crossovers. He was a soldier in the secret skirmishes of the zaibatsus, the multinational corporations that control entire economies.

I see Fox grinning, talking fast, dismissing my ventures into intercorporate espionage with a shake of his head. The Edge, he said, have to find that Edge. He made you hear the capital *E*. The Edge was Fox's grail, that essential fraction of sheer human talent, nontransferable, locked in the skulls of the world's hottest research scientists.

You can't put Edge down on paper, Fox said, can't punch Edge into a diskette.

The money was in corporate defectors.

Fox was smooth, the severity of his dark French suits offset by a boyish forelock that wouldn't stay in place. I never liked the way the effect was ruined when he stepped back from the bar, his left shoulder skewed at an angle no Paris tailor could conceal. Someone had run him over with a taxi in Berne, and nobody quite knew how to put him together again.

I guess I went with him because he said he was after that Edge.

And somewhere out there, on our way to find the Edge, I found you, Sandii.

The New Rose Hotel is a coffin rack on the ragged fringes of Narita International. Plastic capsules a meter high and three long, stacked like surplus Godzilla teeth in a concrete lot off the main road to the airport. Each capsule has a television mounted flush with the ceiling. I spend whole days watching Japanese game shows and old movies. Sometimes I have your gun in my hand.

Sometimes I can hear the jets, laced into holding patterns over Narita. I close my eyes and imagine the sharp, white contrails fading, losing definition.

You walked into a bar in Yokohama, the first time I saw you. Eurasian, half gaijin, long-hipped and fluid in a Chinese knock-off of some Tokyo designer's original. Dark European eyes, Asian cheekbones. I remember you dumping your purse out on the bed, later, in some hotel room, pawing through your makeup. A crumpled wad of new yen, dilapidated address book held together with rubber bands, a Mitsubishi bank chip, Japanese passport with a gold chrysanthemum stamped on the cover, and the Chinese .22.

You told me your story. Your father had been an executive in

Tokyo, but now he was disgraced, disowned, cast down by Hosaka, the biggest zaibatsu of all. That night your mother was Dutch, and I listened as you spun out those summers in Amsterdam for me, the pigeons in Dam Square like a soft, brown carpet.

I never asked what your father might have done to earn his disgrace. I watched you dress; watched the swing of your dark, straight hair, how it cut the air.

Now Hosaka hunts me.

The coffins of New Rose are racked in recycled scaffolding, steel pipes under bright enamel. Paint flakes away when I climb the ladder, falls with each step as I follow the catwalk. My left hand counts off the coffin hatches, their multilingual decals warning of fines levied for the loss of a key.

I look up as the jets rise out of Narita, passage home, distant now as any moon.

Fox was quick to see how we could use you, but not sharp enough to credit you with ambition. But then he never lay all night with you on the beach at Kamakura, never listened to your nightmares, never heard an entire imagined childhood shift under those stars, shift and roll over, your child's mouth opening to reveal some fresh past, and always the one, you swore, that was really and finally the truth.

I didn't care, holding your hips while the sand cooled against your skin.

Once you left me, ran back to that beach saying you'd forgotten our key. I found it in the door and went after you, to find you ankle-deep in surf, your smooth back rigid, trembling; your eyes far away. You couldn't talk. Shivering. Gone. Shaking for different futures and better pasts.

Sandii, you left me here.

You left me all your things.

This gun. Your makeup, all the shadows and blushes capped in plastic. Your Cray microcomputer, a gift from Fox, with a shopping list you entered. Sometimes I play that back, watching each item cross the little silver screen.

A freezer. A fermenter. An incubator. An electrophoresis system with integrated agarose cell and transilluminator. A tissue embedder. A high-performance liquid chromatograph. A flow cytometer. A spectrophotometer. Four gross of borosilicate scintillation vials. A microcentrifuge. And one DNA synthesizer, with in-built computer. Plus software.

Expensive, Sandii, but then Hosaka was footing our bills. Later you made them pay even more, but you were already gone.

Hiroshi drew up that list for you. In bed, probably. Hiroshi Yomiuri. Maas Biolabs GmbH had him. Hosaka wanted him.

He was hot. Edge and lots of it. Fox followed genetic engineers the way a fan follows players in a favorite game. Fox wanted Hiroshi so bad he could taste it.

He'd sent me up to Frankfurt three times before you turned up, just to have a look-see at Hiroshi. Not to make a pass or even to give him a wink and a nod. Just to watch.

Hiroshi showed all the signs of having settled in. He'd found a German girl with a taste for conservative loden and riding boots polished the shade of a fresh chestnut. He'd bought a renovated town house on just the right square. He'd taken up fencing and given up kendo.

And everywhere the Maas security teams, smooth and heavy, a rich, clear syrup of surveillance. I came back and told Fox we'd never touch him.

You touched him for us, Sandii. You touched him just right.

Our Hosaka contacts were like specialized cells protecting the parent organism. We were mutagens, Fox and I, dubious agents adrift on the dark side of the intercorporate sea.

When we had you in place in Vienna, we offered them Hiroshi. They didn't even blink. Dead calm in an L.A. hotel room. They said they had to think about it.

Fox spoke the name of Hosaka's primary competitor in the gene game, let it fall out naked, broke the protocol forbidding the use of proper names.

They had to think about it, they said.

Fox gave them three days.

I took you to Barcelona a week before I took you to Vienna. I remember you with your hair tucked back into a gray beret, your high Mongol cheekbones reflected in the windows of ancient shops. Strolling down the Ramblas to the Phoenician harbor, past the glass-roofed Mercado selling oranges out of Africa.

The old Ritz, warm in our room, dark, with all the soft weight of Europe pulled over us like a quilt. I could enter you in your sleep. You were always ready. Seeing your lips in a soft, round *O* of surprise, your face about to sink into the thick, white pillow—archaic linen of the Ritz. Inside you I imagined all that neon, the crowds surging around Shinjuku Station, wired electric night. You moved that way, rhythm of a new age, dreamy and far from any nation's soil.

When we flew to Vienna, I installed you in Hiroshi's wife's favorite hotel. Quiet, solid, the lobby tiled like a marble chessboard, with brass elevators smelling of lemon oil and small cigars. It was easy to imagine her there, the highlights on her riding boots reflected in polished marble, but we knew she wouldn't be coming along, not this trip.

She was off to some Rhineland spa, and Hiroshi was in Vienna for a conference. When Maas security flowed in to scan the hotel, you were out of sight.

Hiroshi arrived an hour later, alone.

Imagine an alien, Fox once said, who's come here to identify the planet's dominant form of intelligence. The alien has a look, then chooses. What do you think he picks? I probably shrugged.

The zaibatsus, Fox said, the multinationals. The blood of a zaibatsu is information, not people. The structure is independent of the individual lives that comprise it. Corporation as life form.

Not the Edge lecture again, I said.

Maas isn't like that, he said, ignoring me.

Maas was small, fast, ruthless. An atavism. Maas was all Edge.

I remember Fox talking about the nature of Hiroshi's Edge. Radioactive nucleases, monoclonal antibodies, something to do with the linkage of proteins, nucleotides . . . Hot, Fox called them, hot proteins. High-speed links. He said Hiroshi was a freak, the kind who shatters paradigms, inverts a whole field of science, brings on the violent revision of an entire body of knowledge. Basic patents, he said, his throat tight with the sheer wealth of it, with the high, thin smell of tax-free millions that clung to those two words.

Hosaka wanted Hiroshi, but his Edge was radical enough to worry them. They wanted him to work in isolation.

I went to Marrakech, to the old city, the Medina. I found a heroin lab that had been converted to the extraction of pheromones. I bought it, with Hosaka's money.

I walked the marketplace at Djemaa-el-Fna with a sweating Portuguese businessman, discussing fluorescent lighting and the installation of ventilated specimen cages. Beyond the city walls, the high Atlas. Djemaa-el-Fna was thick with jugglers, dancers, storytellers, small boys turning lathes with their feet, legless beggars with wooden bowls under animated holograms advertising French software.

We strolled past bales of raw wool and plastic tubs of Chinese microchips. I hinted that my employers planned to manufacture synthetic beta-endorphin. Always try to give them something they understand.

Sandii, I remember you in Harajuku, sometimes. Close my eyes in this coffin and I can see you there—all the glitter, crystal maze of the boutiques, the smell of new clothes. I see your cheekbones ride past chrome racks of Paris leathers. Sometimes I hold your hand.

We thought we'd found you, Sandii, but really you'd found us. Now I know you were looking for us, or for someone like us. Fox was delighted, grinning over our find: such a pretty new tool, bright as any scalpel. Just the thing to help us sever a stubborn Edge, like Hiroshi's, from the jealous parent-body of Maas Biolabs.

You must have been searching a long time, looking for a way out, all those nights down Shinjuku. Nights you carefully cut from the scattered deck of your past.

My own past had gone down years before, lost with all hands, no trace. I understood Fox's late-night habit of emptying his wallet, shuffling through his identification. He'd lay the pieces out in different patterns, rearrange them, wait for a picture to form. I knew what he was looking for. You did the same thing with your childhoods.

In New Rose, tonight, I choose from your deck of pasts.

I choose the original version, the famous Yokohama hotel-room text, recited to me that first night in bed. I choose the disgraced father, Hosaka executive. Hosaka. How perfect. And the Dutch mother, the summers in Amsterdam, the soft blanket of pigeons in the Dam Square afternoon.

I came in out of the heat of Marrakech into Hilton air-conditioning. Wet shirt clinging cold to the small of my back while I read the message you'd relayed through Fox. You were in all the way; Hiroshi would leave his wife. It wasn't difficult for you to communicate with us, even through the clear, tight film of Maas security; you'd shown Hiroshi the perfect little place for coffee and kipferl. Your favorite waiter was white-haired, kindly, walked with a limp, and worked for us. You left your messages under the linen napkin.

All day today I watched a small helicopter cut a tight grid above this country of mine, the land of my exile, the New Rose Hotel. Watched from my hatch as its patient shadow crossed the grease-stained concrete. Close. Very close.

I left Marrakech for Berlin. I met with a Welshman in a bar and began to arrange for Hiroshi's disappearance.

It would be a complicated business, intricate as the brass gears and sliding mirrors of Victorian stage magic, but the desired effect was simple enough. Hiroshi would step behind a hydrogen-cell Mercedes and vanish. The dozen Maas agents who followed him constantly would swarm around the van like ants; the Maas security apparatus would harden around his point of departure like epoxy.

They know how to do business promptly in Berlin. I was even able to arrange a last night with you. I kept it secret from Fox; he might not have approved. Now I've forgotten the town's name. I knew it for an hour on the autobahn, under a gray Rhenish sky, and forgot it in your arms.

The rain began, sometime toward morning. Our room had a single window, high and narrow, where I stood and watched the rain fur the river with silver needles. Sound of your breathing. The river flowed beneath low, stone arches. The street was empty. Europe was a dead museum.

I'd already booked your flight to Marrakech, out of Orly,

under your newest name. You'd be on your way when I pulled
the final string and dropped Hiroshi out of sight.

You'd left your purse on the dark old bureau. While you slept
I went through your things, removing anything that might clash
with the new cover I'd bought for you in Berlin. I took the Chinese .22, your microcomputer, and your bank chip. I took a new
passport, Dutch, from my bag, a Swiss bank chip in the same
name, and tucked them into your purse.

My hand brushed something flat. I drew it out, held the
thing, a diskette. No labels.

It lay there in the palm of my hand, all that death. Latent,
coded, waiting.

I stood there and watched you breathe, watched your
breasts rise and fall. Saw your lips slightly parted, and in the jut
and fullness of your lower lip the faintest suggestion of bruising.

I put the diskette back into your purse. When I lay down beside you, you rolled against me, waking, on your breath all the
electric night of a new Asia, the future rising in you like a bright
fluid, washing me of everything but the moment. That was your
magic, that you lived outside of history, all now.

And you knew how to take me there.

For the very last time, you took me.

While I was shaving, I heard you empty your makeup into my
bag. I'm Dutch now, you said, I'll want a new look.

Dr. Hiroshi Yomiuri went missing in Vienna, in a quiet street
off Singerstrasse, two blocks from his wife's favorite hotel. On a
clear afternoon in October, in the presence of a dozen expert
witnesses, Dr. Yomiuri vanished.

He stepped through a looking glass. Somewhere, offstage,
the oiled play of Victorian clockwork.

I sat in a hotel room in Geneva and took the Welshman's call.

It was done, Hiroshi down my rabbit hole and headed for Mar-rakech. I poured myself a drink and thought about your legs.

Fox and I met in Narita a day later, in a sushi bar in the JAL terminal. He'd just stepped off an Air Maroc jet, exhausted and triumphant.

Loves it there, he said, meaning Hiroshi. Loves her, he said, meaning you.

I smiled. You'd promised to meet me in Shinjuku in a month.

Your cheap little gun in the New Rose Hotel. The chrome is starting to peel. The machining is clumsy, blurry Chinese stamped into rough steel. The grips are red plastic, molded with a dragon on either side. Like a child's toy.

Fox ate sushi in the JAL terminal, high on what we'd done. The shoulder had been giving him trouble, but he said he didn't care. Money now for better doctors. Money now for everything.

Somehow it didn't seem very important to me, the money we'd gotten from Hosaka. Not that I doubted our new wealth, but that last night with you had left me convinced that it all came to us naturally, in the new order of things, as a function of who and what we were.

Poor Fox. With his blue oxford shirts crisper than ever, his Paris suits darker and richer. Sitting there in JAL, dabbing sushi into a little rectangular tray of green horseradish, he had less than a week to live.

Dark now, and the coffin racks of New Rose are lit all night by floodlights, high on painted metal masts. Nothing here seems to serve its original purpose. Everything is surplus recycled, even the coffins. Forty years ago these plastic capsules were stacked in Tokyo or Yokohama, a modern convenience for trav-eling businessmen. Maybe your father slept in one. When the scaffolding was new, it rose around the shell of some mirrored tower on the Ginza, swarmed over by crews of builders.

The breeze tonight brings the rattle of a pachinko parlor, the smell of stewed vegetables from the pushcarts across the road.

I spread crab-flavored krill paste on orange rice crackers. I can hear the planes.

Those last few days in Tokyo, Fox and I had adjoining suites on the fifty-third floor of the Hyatt. No contact with Hosaka. They paid us, then erased us from official corporate memory.

But Fox couldn't let go. Hiroshi was his baby, his pet project. He'd developed a proprietary, almost fatherly, interest in Hiroshi. He loved him for his Edge. So Fox had me keep in touch with my Portuguese businessman in the Medina, who was willing to keep a very partial eye on Hiroshi's lab for us.

When he phoned, he'd phone from a stall in Djemaa-el-Fna, with a background of wailing vendors and Atlas panpipes. Someone was moving security into Marrakech, he told us. Fox nodded. Hosaka.

After less than a dozen calls, I saw the change in Fox, a tension, a look of abstraction. I'd find him at the window, staring down fifty-three floors into the Imperial gardens, lost in something he wouldn't talk about.

Ask him for a more detailed description, he said, after one particular call. He thought a man our contact had seen entering Hiroshi's lab might be Moenner, Hosaka's leading gene man.

That was Moenner, he said, after the next call. Another call and he thought he'd identified Chedanne, who headed Hosaka's protein team. Neither had been seen outside the corporate arcology in over two years.

By then it was obvious that Hosaka's leading researchers were pooling quietly in the Medina, the black executive Lears whispering into the Marrakech airport on carbon-fiber wings. Fox shook his head. He was a professional, a specialist, and he saw the sudden accumulation of all that prime Hosaka Edge in the Medina as a drastic failure in the zaibatsu's tradecraft.

Christ, he said, pouring himself a Black Label, they've got their whole bio section in there right now. One bomb. He shook his head. One grenade in the right place at the right time . . .

I reminded him of the saturation techniques Hosaka security was obviously employing. Hosaka had lines to the heart of the Diet, and their massive infiltration of agents into Marrakech could only be taking place with the knowledge and cooperation of the Moroccan government.

Hang it up, I said. It's over. You've sold them Hiroshi. Now forget him.

I know what it is, he said. I know. I saw it once before.

He said that there was a certain wild factor in lab work. The edge of Edge, he called it. When a researcher develops a breakthrough, others sometimes find it impossible to duplicate the first researcher's results. This was even more likely with Hiroshi, whose work went against the conceptual grain of his field. The answer, often, was to fly the breakthrough boy from lab to corporate lab for a ritual laying on of hands. A few pointless adjustments in the equipment, and the process would work. Crazy thing, he said, nobody knows why it works that way, but it does. He grinned.

But they're taking a chance, he said. Bastards told us they wanted to isolate Hiroshi, keep him away from their central research thrust. Balls. Bet your ass there's some kind of power struggle going on in Hosaka research. Somebody big's flying his favorites in and rubbing them all over Hiroshi for luck. When Hiroshi shoots the legs out from under genetic engineering, the Medina crowd's going to be ready.

He drank his scotch and shrugged.

Go to bed, he said. You're right, it's over.

I did go to bed, but the phone woke me. Marrakech again, the white static of a satellite link, a rush of frightened Portuguese.

Hosaka didn't freeze our credit, they caused it to evaporate. Fairy gold. One minute we were millionaires in the world's hardest currency, and the next we were paupers. I woke Fox.

Sandii, he said. She sold out. Maas security turned her in Vienna. Sweet Jesus.

I watched him slit his battered suitcase apart with a Swiss Army knife. He had three gold bars glued in there with contact cement. Soft plates, each one proofed and stamped by the treasury of some extinct African government.

I should've seen it, he said, his voice flat.

I said no. I think I said your name.

Forget her, he said. Hosaka wants us dead. They'll assume we crossed them. Get on the phone and check our credit.

Our credit was gone. They denied that either of us had ever had an account.

Haul ass, Fox said.

We ran. Out a service door, into Tokyo traffic, and down into Shinjuku. That was when I understood for the first time the real extent of Hosaka's reach.

Every door was closed. People we'd done business with for two years saw us coming, and I'd see steel shutters slam behind their eyes. We'd get out before they had a chance to reach for the phone. The surface tension of the underworld had been tripled, and everywhere we'd meet that same taut membrane and be thrown back. No chance to sink, to get out of sight.

Hosaka let us run for most of that first day. Then they sent someone to break Fox's back a second time.

I didn't see them do it, but I saw him fall. We were in a Ginza department store an hour before closing, and I saw his arc off that polished mezzanine, down into all the wares of the new Asia.

They missed me somehow, and I just kept running. Fox took the gold with him, but I had a hundred new yen in my pocket. I ran. All the way to the New Rose Hotel.

Now it's time.

Come with me, Sandii. Hear the neon humming on the road to Narita International. A few late moths trace stop-motion circles around the floodlights that shine on New Rose.

And the funny thing, Sandii, is how sometimes you just don't seem real to me. Fox once said you were ectoplasm, a ghost called up by the extremes of economics. Ghost of the new century, congealing on a thousand beds in the world's Hyatts, the world's Hiltons.

Now I've got your gun in my hand, jacket pocket, and my hand seems so far away. Disconnected.

I remember my Portuguese business friend forgetting his English, trying to get it across in four languages I barely understood, and I thought he was telling me that the Medina was burning. Not the Medina. The brains of Hosaka's best research people. Plague, he was whispering, my businessman, plague and fever and death.

Smart Fox, he put it together on the run. I didn't even have to mention finding the diskette in your bag in Germany.

Someone had reprogrammed the DNA synthesizer, he said. The thing was there for the overnight construction of just the right macromolecule. With its in-built computer and its custom software. Expensive, Sandii. But not as expensive as you turned out to be for Hosaka.

I hope you got a good price from Maas.

The diskette in my hand. Rain on the river. I knew, but I couldn't face it. I put the code for that meningeal virus back into your purse and lay down beside you.

So Moenner died, along with other Hosaka researchers. Including Hiroshi. Chedanne suffered permanent brain damage.

Hiroshi hadn't worried about contamination. The proteins he punched for were harmless. So the synthesizer hummed to itself all night long, building a virus to the specifications of Maas Biolabs GmbH.

Maas. Small, fast, ruthless. All Edge.

The airport road is a long, straight shot. Keep to the shadows.

And I was shouting at that Portuguese voice, I made him tell me what happened to the girl, to Hiroshi's woman. Vanished, he said. The whir of Victorian clockwork.

So Fox had to fall, fall with his three pathetic plates of gold, and snap his spine for the last time. On the floor of a Ginza department store, every shopper staring in the instant before they screamed.

I just can't hate you, baby.

And Hosaka's helicopter is back, no lights at all, hunting on infrared, feeling for body heat. A muffled whine as it turns, a kilometer away, swinging back toward us, toward New Rose. Too fast a shadow, against the glow of Narita.

It's all right, baby. Only please come here. Hold my hand.

it rains a lot up here; there are winter days when it doesn't really get light at all, only a bright, indeterminate gray. But then there are days when it's like they whip aside a curtain to flash you three minutes of sunlit, suspended mountain, the trademark at the start of God's own movie. It was like that the day her agents phoned, from deep in the heart of their mirrored pyramid on Beverly Boulevard, to tell me she'd merged with the net, crossed over for good, that *Kings of Sleep* was going triple-platinum. I'd edited most of *Kings,* done the brain-map work and gone over it all with the fast-wipe module, so I was in line for a share of royalties.

No, I said, no. Then yes, yes, and hung up on them. Got my jacket and took the stairs three at a time, straight out to the nearest bar and an eight-hour blackout that ended on a concrete ledge two meters above midnight. False Creek water. City lights, that same gray bowl of sky smaller now, illuminated by neon and mercury-vapor arcs. And it was snowing, big flakes but not many, and when they touched black water, they were gone, no trace at all. I looked down at my feet and saw my toes clear of the edge of concrete, the water between them. I was wearing Japanese shoes, new and expensive, glove-leather Ginza monkey boots with rubber-capped toes. I stood there for a long time before I took that first step back.

Because she was dead, and I'd let her go. Because, now, she

was immortal, and I'd helped her get that way. And because I knew she'd phone me, in the morning.

my father was an audio engineer, a mastering engineer. He went way back, in the business, even before digital. The processes he was concerned with were partly mechanical, with that clunky quasi-Victorian quality you see in twentieth-century technology. He was a lathe operator, basically. People brought him audio recordings and he burned their sounds into grooves on a disk of lacquer. Then the disk was electroplated and used in the construction of a press that would stamp out records, the black things you see in antique stores. And I remember him telling me, once, a few months before he died, that certain frequencies—transients, I think he called them—could easily burn out the head, the cutting head, on a master lathe. These heads were incredibly expensive, so you prevented burnouts with something called an accelerometer. And that was what I was thinking of, as I stood there, my toes out over the water: that head, burning out.

Because that was what they did to her.

And that was what she wanted.

No accelerometer for Lise.

i disconnected my phone on my way to bed. I did it with the business end of a West German studio tripod that was going to cost a week's wages to repair.

Woke some strange time later and took a cab back to Granville Island and Rubin's place.

Rubin, in some way that no one quite understands, is a master, a teacher, what the Japanese call a *sensei*. What he's the master of, really, is garbage, kipple, refuse, the sea of cast-off goods our century floats on. *Gomi no sensei*. Master of junk.

I found him, this time, squatting between two vicious-looking drum machines I hadn't seen before, rusty spider arms folded at the hearts of dented constellations of steel cans fished out of Richmond dumpsters. He never calls the place a studio, never refers to himself as an artist. "Messing around," he calls what he does there, and seems to view it as some extension of boyhood's perfectly bored backyard afternoons. He wanders through his jammed, littered space, a kind of minihangar cobbled to the water side of the Market, followed by the smarter and more agile of his creations, like some vaguely benign Satan bent on the elaboration of still stranger processes in his ongoing Inferno of *gomi*. I've seen Rubin program his constructions to identify and verbally abuse pedestrians wearing garments by a given season's hot designer; others attend to more obscure missions, and a few seem constructed solely to deconstruct themselves with as much attendant noise as possible. He's like a child, Rubin; he's also worth a lot of money in galleries in Tokyo and Paris.

So I told him about Lise. He let me do it, get it out, then nodded. "I know," he said. "Some CBC creep phoned eight times." He sipped something out of a dented cup. "You wanna Wild Turkey sour?"

"Why'd they call you?"

" 'Cause my name's on the back of *Kings of Sleep*. Dedication."

"I didn't see it yet."

"She try to call you yet?"

"No."

"She will."

"Rubin, she's dead. They cremated her already."

"I know," he said. "And she's going to call you."

gomi.

Where does the *gomi* stop and the world begin? The Japanese, a century ago, had already run out of *gomi* space around Tokyo, so they came up with a plan for creating space out of *gomi*. By the year 1969 they had built themselves a little island in Tokyo Bay, out of *gomi*, and christened it Dream Island. But the city was still pouring out its nine thousand tons per day, so they went on to build New Dream Island, and today they coordinate the whole process, and new Nippons rise out of the Pacific. Rubin watches this on the news and says nothing at all.

He has nothing to say about *gomi*. It's his medium, the air he breathes, something he's swum in all his life. He cruises Greater Van in a spavined truck-thing chopped down from an ancient Mercedes airporter, its roof lost under a wallowing rubber bag half-filled with natural gas. He looks for things that fit some strange design scrawled on the inside of his forehead by whatever serves him as Muse. He brings home more *gomi*. Some of it still operative. Some of it, like Lise, human.

I met Lise at one of Rubin's parties. Rubin had a lot of parties. He never seemed particularly to enjoy them, himself, but they were excellent parties. I lost track, that fall, of the number of times I woke on a slab of foam to the roar of Rubin's antique espresso machine, a tarnished behemoth topped with a big chrome eagle, the sound outrageous off the corrugated steel walls of the place, but massively comforting, too: There was coffee. Life would go on.

First time I saw her: in the Kitchen Zone. You wouldn't call it a kitchen, exactly, just three fridges and a hot plate and a broken convection oven that had come in with the *gomi*. First time I saw her: She had the all-beer fridge open, light spilling out, and I caught the cheekbones and the determined set of that mouth, but I also caught the black glint of polycarbon at her wrist, and the bright slick sore the exoskeleton had rubbed there. Too drunk to process, to know what it was, but I did know it wasn't party time. So I did what people usually did, to Lise, and clicked myself into a different movie. Went for the wine instead, on the counter beside the convection oven. Never looked back.

But she found me again. Came after me two hours later, weaving through the bodies and junk with that terrible grace programmed into the exoskeleton. I knew what it was, then, as I watched her homing in, too embarrassed now to duck it, to run, to mumble some excuse and get out. Pinned there, my arm around the waist of a girl I didn't know, while Lise advanced—*was advanced,* with that mocking grace—straight at me now, her eyes burning with wizz, and the girl had wriggled out and away in a quiet social panic, was gone, and Lise stood there in front of me, propped up in her pencil-thin polycarbon prosthetic. Looked into those eyes and it was like you could hear her synapses whining, some impossibly high-pitched scream as the wizz opened every circuit in her brain.

"Take me home," she said, and the words hit me like a whip. I think I shook my head. "Take me home." There were levels of pain there, and subtlety, and an amazing cruelty. And I knew then that I'd never been hated, ever, as deeply or thoroughly as this wasted little girl hated me now, hated me for the way I'd looked, then looked away, beside Rubin's all-beer refrigerator.

So—if that's the word—I did one of those things you do and never find out why, even though something in you knows you could never have done anything else.

I took her home.

———

i have two rooms in an old condo rack at the corner of Fourth and MacDonald, tenth floor. The elevators usually work, and if you sit on the balcony railing and lean out backward, holding on to the corner of the building next door, you can see a little up-right slit of sea and mountain.

She hadn't said a word, all the way back from Rubin's, and I was getting sober enough to feel very uneasy as I unlocked the door and let her in.

The first thing she saw was the portable fast-wipe I'd brought home from the Pilot the night before. The exoskeleton carried her across the dusty broadloom with that same walk, like a model down a runway. Away from the crash of the party, I could hear it click softly as it moved her. She stood there, looking down at the fast-wipe. I could see the thing's ribs when she stood like that, make them out across her back through the scuffed black leather of her jacket. One of those diseases. Either one of the old ones they've never quite figured out or one of the new ones—the all too obviously environmental kind—that they've barely even named yet. She couldn't move, not without that extra skeleton, and it was jacked straight into her brain, myoelectric interface. The fragile-looking polycarbon braces moved her arms and legs, but a more subtle system handled her thin hands, galvanic inlays. I thought of frog legs twitching in a high-school lab tape, then hated myself for it.

"This is a fast-wipe module," she said, in a voice I hadn't heard before, distant, and I thought then that the wizz might be wearing off. "What's it doing here?"

"I edit," I said, closing the door behind me.

"Well, now," and she laughed. "You do. Where?"

"On the Island. Place called the Autonomic Pilot."

She turned; then, hand on thrust hip, she swung—it swung her—and the wizz and the hate and some terrible parody of lust stabbed out at me from those washed-out gray eyes. "You wanna make it, editor?"

And I felt the whip come down again, but I wasn't going to take it, not again. So I cold-eyed her from somewhere down in the beer-numb core of my walking, talking, live-limbed, and entirely ordinary body and the words came out of me like spit: "Could you feel it, if I did?"

Beat. Maybe she blinked, but her face never registered. "No," she said "but sometimes I like to watch."

rubin stands at the window, two days after her death in Los Angeles, watching snow fall into False Creek. "So you never went to bed with her?"

One of his push-me-pull-you's, little roller-bearing Escher lizards, scoots across the table in front of me, in curl-up mode.

"No," I say, and it's true. Then I laugh. "But we jacked straight across. That first night."

"You were crazy," he said, a certain approval in his voice. "It might have killed you. Your heart might have stopped, you might have stopped breathing. . . ." He turns back to the window. "Has she called you yet?"

we jacked, straight across.

I'd never done it before. If you'd asked me why, I would have told you that I was an editor and that it wasn't professional.

The truth would be something more like this.

In the trade, the legitimate trade—I've never done porno— we call the raw product dry dreams. Dry dreams are neural output from levels of consciousness that most people can only access in sleep. But artists, the kind I work with at the Autonomic Pilot, are able to break the surface tension, dive down deep, down and out, out into Jung's sea, and bring back—well, dreams. Keep it simple. I guess some artists have always done that, in whatever medium, but neuroelectronics lets us access the experience, and the net gets it all out on the wire, so we can package it, sell it, watch how it moves in the market. Well, the more things change . . . That's something my father liked to say.

Ordinarily I get the raw material in a studio situation, filtered through several million dollars' worth of baffles, and I don't even have to see the artist. The stuff we get out to the consumer, you see, has been structured, balanced, turned into art. There are still people naive enough to assume that they'll actually enjoy jacking straight across with someone they love. I think most teenagers try it, once. Certainly it's easy enough to do; Radio Shack will sell you the box and the trodes and the cables. But me, I'd never done it. And now that I think about it, I'm not so sure I can explain why. Or that I even want to try.

I do know why I did it with Lise, sat down beside her on my Mexican futon and snapped the optic lead into the socket on the spine, the smooth dorsal ridge, of the exoskeleton. It was high up, at the base of her neck, hidden by her dark hair.

Because she claimed she was an artist, and because I knew that we were engaged, somehow, in total combat, and I was *not* going to lose. That may not make sense to you, but then you never knew her, or know her through *Kings of Sleep*, which isn't the same at all. You never felt that hunger she had, which was pared down to a dry need, hideous in its singleness of purpose. People who know *exactly* what they want have always frightened me, and Lise had known what she wanted for a long time, and wanted nothing else at all. And I was scared, then, of admitting to myself that I was scared, and I'd seen enough strangers' dreams, in the mixing room at the Autonomic Pilot, to know that most people's inner monsters are foolish things, ludicrous in the calm light of one's own consciousness. And I was still drunk.

I put the trodes on and reached for the stud on the fast-wipe. I'd shut down its studio functions, temporarily converting eighty thousand dollars' worth of Japanese electronics to the equivalent of one of those little Radio Shack boxes. "Hit it," I said, and touched the switch.

Words. Words cannot. Or, maybe, just barely, if I even knew how to begin to describe it, what came up out of her, what she did . . .

There's a segment on *Kings of Sleep*; it's like you're on a motorcycle at midnight, no lights but somehow you don't need them, blasting out along a cliff-high stretch of coast highway, so fast that you hang there in a cone of silence, the bike's thunder lost behind you. Everything, lost behind you. . . . It's just a blink, on *Kings*, but it's one of the thousand things you remember, go back to, incorporate into your own vocabulary of feelings. Amazing. Freedom and death, right there, right there, razor's edge, forever.

What I got was the big-daddy version of that, raw rush, the king hell killer uncut real thing, exploding eight ways from Sunday into a void that stank of poverty and lovelessness and obscurity.

And that was Lise's ambition, that rush, *seen from the inside*.

It probably took all of four seconds.

And, of course, she'd won.

I took the trodes off and stared at the wall, eyes wet, the framed posters swimming.

I couldn't look at her. I heard her disconnect the optic lead. I heard the exoskeleton creak as it hoisted her up from the futon. Heard it tick demurely as it hauled her into the kitchen for a glass of water.

Then I started to cry.

rubin inserts a skinny probe in the roller-bearing belly of a sluggish push-me-pull-you and peers at the circuitry through magnifying glasses with miniature headlights mounted at the temples.

"So? You got hooked." He shrugs, looks up. It's dark now and the twin tensor beams stab at my face, chill damp in his steel barn and the lonesome hoot of a foghorn from somewhere across the water. "So?"

My turn to shrug. "I just did. . . . There didn't seem to be anything else to do."

The beams duck back to the silicon heart of his defective toy. "Then you're okay. It was a true choice. What I mean is, she was set to be what she is. You had about as much to do with where she's at today as that fast-wipe module did. She'd have found somebody else if she hadn't found you."

i made a deal with Barry, the senior editor, got twenty minutes at five on a cold September morning. Lise came in and hit me with that same shot, but this time I was ready, with my baffles and brain maps, and I didn't have to feel it. It took me two weeks, piecing out the minutes in the editing room, to cut what she'd done down into something I could play for Max Bell, who owns the Pilot.

Bell hadn't been happy, not happy at all, as I explained what I'd done. Maverick editors can be a problem, and eventually most editors decide that they've found someone who'll be it, the next monster, and then they start wasting time and money. He'd nodded when I'd finished my pitch, then scratched his nose with the cap of his red felt pen. "Uh-huh. Got it. Hottest thing since fish grew legs, right?"

But he'd jacked it, the demo soft I'd put together, and when it clicked out of its slot in his Braun desk unit, he was staring at the wall, his face blank.

"Max?"

"Huh?"

"What do you think?"

'Think? I . . . What did you say her name was?" He blinked. "Lisa? Who you say she's signed with?"

"Lise. Nobody, Max. She hasn't signed with anybody yet."

"Jesus Christ." He still looked blank.

"you know how I found her?" Rubin asks, wading through ragged cardboard boxes to find the light switch. The boxes are filled with carefully sorted *gomi*: lithium batteries, tantalum capacitors, RF connectors, breadboards, barrier strips, ferroresonant transformers, spools of bus bar wire. . . . One box is filled with the severed heads of hundreds of Barbie dolls, another with armored industrial safety gauntlets that look like spacesuit gloves. Light floods the room and a sort of Kandinski mantis in snipped and painted tin swings its golfball-size head toward the bright bulb. "I was down Granville on a *gomi* run, back in an alley, and I found her just sitting there. Caught the skeleton and she didn't look so good, so I asked her if she was okay. Nothin'. Just closed her eyes. Not my lookout, I think. But I happen back by there about four hours later and she hasn't moved. 'Look, honey,' I tell her, 'maybe your hardware's buggered up. I can help you, okay?' Nothin'. 'How long you been back here?'

Nothin'. So I take off." He crosses to his workbench and strokes the thin metal limbs of the mantis thing with a pale forefinger. Behind the bench, hung on damp-swollen sheets of ancient pegboard, are pliers, screwdrivers, tie-wrap guns, a rusted Daisy BB rifle, coax strippers, crimpers, logic probes, heat guns, a pocket oscilloscope, seemingly every tool in human history, with no attempt ever made to order them at all, though I've yet to see Rubin's hand hesitate.

"So I went back," he says. "Gave it an hour. She was out by then, unconscious, so I brought her back here and ran a check on the exoskeleton. Batteries were dead. She'd crawled back there when the juice ran out and settled down to starve to death, I guess."

"When was that?"

"About a week before you took her home."

"But what if she'd died? If you hadn't found her?"

"Somebody was going to find her. She couldn't *ask* for anything, you know? Just *take*. Couldn't stand a favor."

max found the agents for her, and a trio of awesomely slick junior partners Leared into YVR a day later. Lise wouldn't come down to the Pilot to meet them, insisted we bring them up to Rubin's, where she still slept.

"Welcome to Couverville," Rubin said as they edged in the door. His long face was smeared with grease, the fly of his ragged fatigue pants held more or less shut with a twisted paper clip. The boys grinned automatically, but there was something marginally more authentic about the girl's smile. "Mr. Stark," she said, "I was in London last week. I saw your installation at the Tate."

"*Marcello's Battery Factory*," Rubin said. "They say it's scatological, the Brits. . . ." He shrugged. "Brits. I mean, who knows?"

"They're right. It's also very funny."

The boys were beaming like tabled-tanned lighthouses, standing there in their suits. The demo had reached Los Angeles. They knew.

"And you're Lise," she said, negotiating the path between Rubin's heaped *gomi*. "You're going to be a very famous person soon, Lise. We have a lot to discuss. . . ."

And Lise just stood there, propped in polycarbon, and the look on her face was the one I'd seen that first night, in my condo, when she'd asked me if I wanted to go to bed. But if the junior agent lady saw it, she didn't show it. She was a pro.

I told myself that I was a pro, too.

I told myself to relax.

trash fires gutter in steel canisters around the Market. The snow still falls and kids huddle over the flames like arthritic crows, hopping from foot to foot, wind whipping their dark coats. Up in Fairview's arty slum-tumble, someone's laundry has frozen solid on the line, pink squares of bedsheet standing out against the background dinge and the confusion of satellite dishes and solar panels. Some ecologist's eggbeater windmill goes round and round, round and round, giving a whirling finger to the Hydro rates.

Rubin clumps along in paint-spattered L. L. Bean gumshoes, his big head pulled down into an oversize fatigue jacket. Sometimes one of the hunched teens will point him out as we pass, the guy who builds all the crazy stuff, the robots and shit.

"You know what your trouble is?" he says when we're under

the bridge, headed up to Fourth. "You're the kind who *always reads the handbook*. Anything people build, any kind of technology, it's going to have some specific purpose. It's for doing something that somebody already understands. But if it's new technology, it'll open areas nobody's ever thought of before. You read the manual, man, and you won't play around with it, not the same way. And you get all funny when somebody else uses it to do something you never thought of. Like Lise."

"She wasn't the first." Traffic drums past overhead.

"No, but she's sure as hell the first person *you* ever met who went and translated themself into a hardwired program. You lose any sleep when whatsisname did it, three-four years ago, the French kid, the writer?"

"I didn't really think about it, much. A gimmick. PR . . ."

"He's still writing. The weird thing is, he's going to *be* writing, unless somebody blows up his mainframe. . . ."

I wince, shake my head. "But it's not *him*, is it? It's just a program."

"Interesting point. Hard to say. With Lise, though, we find out. She's not a writer."

she had it all in there, *Kings*, locked up in her head the way her body was locked in that exoskeleton.

The agents signed her with a label and brought in a production team from Tokyo. She told them she wanted me to edit. I said no; Max dragged me into his office and threatened to fire me on the spot. If I wasn't involved, there was no reason to do the studio work at the Pilot. Vancouver was hardly the center of the world, and the agents wanted her in Los Angeles. It meant a lot of money to him, and it might put the Autonomic Pilot on the map. I couldn't explain to him why I'd refused. It was too crazy, too personal; she was getting a final dig in. Or that's what I thought then. But Max was serious. He really didn't give me any choice. We both knew another job wasn't going to crawl into my hand. I went back out with him and we told the agents that we'd worked it out: I was on.

The agents showed us lots of teeth.

Lise pulled out an inhaler full of wizz and took a huge hit. I thought I saw the agent lady raise one perfect eyebrow, but that was the extent of censure. After the papers were signed, Lise more or less did what she wanted.

And Lise always knew what she wanted.

We did *Kings* in three weeks, the basic recording. I found any number of reasons to avoid Rubin's place, even believed some of them myself. She was still staying there, although the agents weren't too happy with what they saw as a total lack of security. Rubin told me later that he'd had to have *his* agent call them up and raise hell, but after that they seemed to quit worrying. I hadn't known that Rubin had an agent. It was always easy to forget that Rubin Stark was more famous, then, than anyone else I knew, certainly more famous than I thought Lise was ever likely to become. I knew we were working on something strong, but you never know how big anything's liable to be.

But the time I spent in the Pilot, I was *on*. Lise was amazing.

It was like she was born to the form, even though the technology that made that form possible hadn't even existed when she was born. You see something like that and you wonder how many thousands, maybe millions, of phenomenal artists have died mute, down the centuries, people who could never have been poets or painters or saxophone players, but who had this stuff inside, these psychic waveforms waiting for the circuitry required to tap in. . . .

I learned a few things about her, incidentals, from our time in the studio. That she was born in Windsor. That her father was American and served in Peru and came home crazy and half-blind. That whatever was wrong with her body was congenital. That she had those sores because she refused to remove the ex-oskeleton, ever, because she'd start to choke and die at the thought of that utter helplessness. That she was addicted to wizz and doing enough of it daily to wire a football team.

Her agents brought in medics, who padded the polycarbon with foam and sealed the sores over with micropore dressings. They pumped her up with vitamins and tried to work on her diet, but nobody ever tried to take that inhaler away.

They brought in hairdressers and makeup artists, too, and wardrobe people and image builders and articulate little PR hamsters, and she endured it with something that might almost have been a smile.

And, right through those three weeks, we didn't talk. Just studio talk, artist-editor stuff, very much a restricted code. Her imagery was so strong, so extreme, that she never really needed to explain a given effect to me. I took what she put out and worked with it, and jacked it back to her. She'd either say yes or no, and usually it was yes. The agents noted this and approved, and clapped Max Bell on the back and took him out to dinner, and my salary went up.

And I was pro, all the way. Helpful and thorough and polite. I was determined not to crack again, and never thought about the night I cried, and I was also doing the best work I'd ever done, and knew it, and that's a high in itself.

And then, one morning, about six, after a long, long session—when she'd first gotten that eerie cotillion sequence out, the one the kids call the Ghost Dance—she spoke to me. One of the two agent boys had been there, showing teeth, but he was gone now and the Pilot was dead quiet, just the hum of a blower somewhere down by Max's office.

"Casey," she said, her voice hoarse with the wizz, "sorry I hit on you so hard."

I thought for a minute she was telling me something about the recording we'd just made. I looked up and saw her there, and it struck me that we were alone, and hadn't been alone since we'd made the demo.

I had no idea at all what to say. Didn't even know what I felt.

Propped up in the exoskeleton, she was looking worse than she had that first night, at Rubin's. The wizz was eating her, under the stuff the makeup team kept smoothing on, and sometimes it was like seeing a death's-head surface beneath the face of a not very handsome teenager. I had no idea of her real age. Not old, not young.

"The ramp effect," I said, coiling a length of cable.

"What's that?"

"Nature's way of telling you to clean up your act. Sort of mathematical law, says you can only get off real good on a stimulant x number of times, even if you increase the doses. But you can't *ever* get off as nice as you did the first few times. Or you shouldn't be able to, anyway. That's the trouble with designer drugs; they're too clever. That stuff you're doing has some tricky tail on one of its molecules, keeps you from turning the decomposed adrenaline into adrenochrome. If it didn't, you'd be schizophrenic by now. You got any little problems, Lise? Like apnea? Sometimes maybe you stop breathing if you go to sleep?"

But I wasn't even sure I felt the anger that I heard in my own voice.

She stared at me with those pale gray eyes. The wardrobe people had replaced her thrift-shop jacket with a butter-tanned matte black blouson that did a better job of hiding the polycarbon ribs. She kept it zipped to the neck, always, even though it was too warm in the studio. The hairdressers had tried something new the day before, and it hadn't worked out, her rough dark hair a lopsided explosion above that drawn, triangular face. She stared at me and I felt it again, her singleness of purpose.

"I don't sleep, Casey."

It wasn't until later, much later, that I remembered she'd told me she was sorry. She never did again, and it was the only time I ever heard her say anything that seemed to be out of character.

rubin's diet consists of vending-machine sandwiches, Pakistani takeout food, and espresso. I've never seen him eat anything else. We eat samosas in a narrow shop on Fourth that has a single plastic table wedged between the counter and the door to the can. Rubin eats his dozen samosas, six meat and six veggie, with total concentration, one after another, and doesn't bother to wipe his chin. He's devoted to the place. He loathes the Greek counterman; it's mutual, a real relationship. If the counterman left, Rubin might not come back. The Greek glares at the crumbs on Rubin's chin and jacket. Between samosas, he shoots daggers right back, his eyes narrowed behind the smudged lenses of his steel-rimmed glasses.

The samosas are dinner. Breakfast will be egg salad on dead white bread, packed in one of those triangles of milky plastic, on top of six little cups of poisonously strong espresso.

"You didn't see it coming, Casey." He peers at me out of the thumbprinted depths of his glasses. " 'Cause you're no good at lateral thinking. You read the handbook. What else did you think she was after? Sex? More wizz? A world tour? She was past all that. That's what made her so strong. She was past it. That's why *Kings of Sleep*'s as big as it is, and why the kids buy it, why they *believe* it. They know. Those kids back down the Market, warming their butts around the fires and wondering if they'll find someplace to sleep tonight, they believe it. It's the hottest soft in eight years. Guy at a shop on Granville told me he gets more of the damned things lifted than he sells of anything else. Says it's a hassle to even stock it. . . . She's big because she was what they are, only more so. She knew, man. No dreams, no hope. You can't see the cages on those kids, Casey, but more and more they're twigging to it, that they aren't going *anywhere*." He brushes a greasy crumb of meat from his chin, missing three more. "So she sang it for them, said it that way they can't, painted them a picture. And she used the money to buy herself a way out, that's all."

I watch the steam bead roll down the window in big drops, streaks in the condensation. Beyond the window I can make out a partially stripped Lada, wheels scavenged, axles down on the pavement.

"How many people have done it, Rubin? Have any idea?"

"Not too many. Hard to say, anyway, because a lot of them are probably politicians we think of as being comfortably and reliably dead." He gives me a funny look. "Not a nice thought. Anyway, they had first shot at the technology. It still costs too much for any ordinary dozen millionaires, but I've heard of at least seven. They say Mitsubishi did it to Weinberg before his immune system finally went tits up. He was head of their hybridoma lab in Okayama. Well, their stock's still pretty high, in monoclonals, so maybe it's true. And Langlais, the French kid, the novelist . . ." He shrugs. "Lise didn't have the money for it. Wouldn't now, even. But she put herself in the right place at the right time. She was about to croak, she was in Hollywood, and they could already see what *Kings* was going to do."

the day we finished up, the band stepped off a JAL shuttle out of London, four skinny kids who operated like a well-oiled machine and displayed a hypertrophied fashion sense and a total lack of affect. I set them up in a row at the Pilot, in identical white Ikea office chairs, smeared saline paste on their temples, taped the trodes on, and ran the rough version of what was going to become *Kings of Sleep*. When they came out of it, they all started talking at once, ignoring me totally, in the British version of that secret language all studio musicians speak, four sets of pale hands zooming and chopping the air.

I could catch enough of it to decide that they were excited. That they thought it was good. So I got my jacket and left. They could wipe their own saline paste off, thanks.

And that night I saw Lise for the last time, though I didn't plan to.

walking back down to the Market, Rubin noisily digesting his meal, red taillights reflected on wet cobbles, the city beyond the Market a clean sculpture of light, a lie, where the broken and the lost burrow into the *gomi* that grows like humus at the bases of the towers of glass ...

"I gotta go to Frankfurt tomorrow, do an installation. You wanna come? I could write you off as a technician." He shrugs his way deeper into the fatigue jacket. "Can't pay you, but you can have airfare, you want ..."

Funny offer, from Rubin, and I know it's because he's worried about me, thinks I'm too strange about Lise, and it's the only thing he can think of, getting me out of town.

"It's colder in Frankfurt now than it is here."

"You maybe need a change, Casey. I dunno . . ."

"Thanks, but Max has a lot of work lined up. Pilot's a big deal now, people flying in from all over . . ."

"Sure."

WHEN I left the band at the Pilot, I went home. Walked up to Fourth and took the trolley home, past the windows of the shops I see every day, each one lit up jazzy and slick, clothes and shoes and software, Japanese motorcycles crouched like clean enamel scorpions, Italian furniture. The windows change with the seasons, the shops come and go. We were into the preholiday mode now, and there were more people on the street, a lot of couples, walking quickly and purposefully past the bright windows, on their way to score that perfect little whatever for whomever, half the girls in those padded thigh-high nylon boot things that came out of New York the winter before, the ones that Rubin said made them look like they had elephantiasis. I grinned, thinking about that, and suddenly it hit me that it really was over, that I was done with Lise, and that now she'd be sucked off to Hollywood as inexorably as if she'd poked her toe into a black hole, drawn by the unthinkable gravitic tug of Big Money. Believing that, that she was gone—probably *was* gone, by then—I let down some kind of guard in myself and felt the edges of my pity. But just the edges, because I didn't want my evening screwed up by anything. I wanted partytime. It had been a while.

Got off at my corner and the elevator worked on the first try. Good sign, I told myself. Upstairs, I undressed and showered, found a clean shirt, microwaved burritos. Feel normal, I advised my reflection while I shaved. You have been working too hard. Your credit cards have gotten fat. Time to remedy that.

The burritos tasted like cardboard, but I decided I liked them because they were so aggressively normal. My car was in Burnaby, having its leaky hydrogen cell repacked, so I wasn't going to have to worry about driving. I could go out, find party-time, and phone in sick in the morning. Max wasn't going to kick; I was his star boy. He owed me.

You owe me, Max, I said to the subzero bottle of Moskovskaya I fished out of the freezer. Do you ever owe me. I have just spent three weeks editing the dreams and nightmares of one very screwed up person, Max. On your behalf. So that you can grow and prosper, Max. I poured three fingers of vodka into a plastic glass left over from a party I'd thrown the year before and went back into the living room.

Sometimes it looks to me like nobody in particular lives there. Not that it's that messy; I'm a good if somewhat robotic housekeeper, and even remember to dust the tops of framed posters and things, but I have these times when the place abruptly gives me a kind of low-grade chill, with its basic accumulation of basic consumer goods. I mean, it's not like I want to fill it up with cats or houseplants or anything, but there are moments when I see that anyone could be living there, could own those things, and it all seems sort of interchangeable, my life and yours, my life and anybody's. . . .

I think Rubin sees things that way, too, all the time, but for him it's a source of strength. He lives in other people's garbage, and everything he drags home must have been new and shiny once, must have meant something, however briefly, to someone. So he sweeps it all up into his crazy-looking truck and hauls it back to his place and lets it compost there until he thinks of something new to do with it. Once he was showing me a book of twentieth-century art he liked, and there was a picture of an automated sculpture called *Dead Birds Fly Again,* a thing that whirled real dead birds around and around on a string, and he smiled and nodded, and I could see he felt the artist was a spiritual ancestor of some kind. But what could Rubin do with my framed posters and my Mexican futon from the Bay and my temperfoam bed from Ikea? Well, I thought, taking a first chilly sip, he'd be able to think of something, which was why he was a famous artist and I wasn't.

I went and pressed my forehead against the plate-glass window, as cold as the glass in my hand. Time to go, I said to myself. You are exhibiting symptoms of urban singles angst. There are cures for this. Drink up. Go.

I didn't attain a state of partytime that night. Neither did I exhibit adult common sense and give up, go home, watch some ancient movie, and fall asleep on my futon. The tension those three weeks had built up in me drove me like the mainspring of a mechanical watch, and I went ticking off through nighttown, lubricating my more or less random progress with more drinks. It was one of those nights, I quickly decided, when you slip into an alternate continuum, a city that looks exactly like the one where you live, except for the peculiar difference that it contains not one person you love or know or have even spoken to before. Nights like that, you can go into a familiar bar and find that the staff has just been replaced; then you understand that your real motive in going there was simply to see a familiar face, on a waitress or a bartender, whoever. . . . This sort of thing has been known to mediate against partytime.

I kept it rolling, though, through six or eight places, and eventually it rolled me into a West End club that looked as if it hadn't been redecorated since the Nineties. A lot of peeling chrome over plastic, blurry holograms that gave you a headache

if you tried to make them out. I think Barry had told me about
the place, but I can't imagine why. I looked around and grinned.
If I was looking to be depressed, I'd come to the right place. Yes,
I told myself as I took a corner stool at the bar, this was genuinely sad, really the pits. Dreadful enough to halt the momen-
tum of my shitty evening, which was undoubtedly a good thing.
I'd have one more for the road, admire the grot, and then cab it
on home.

And then I saw Lise.

She hadn't seen me, not yet, and I still had my coat on, tweed
collar up against the weather. She was down the bar and around
the corner with a couple of empty drinks in front of her, big
ones, the kind that come with little Hong Kong parasols or plastic mermaids in them, and as she looked up at the boy beside
her, I saw the wizz flash in her eyes and knew that those drinks
had never contained alcohol, because the levels of drug she was
running couldn't tolerate the mix. The kid, though, was gone,
numb grinning drunk and about ready to slide off his stool, and
running on about something as he made repeated attempts to
focus his eyes and get a better look at Lise, who sat there with
her wardrobe team's black leather blouson zipped to her chin
and her skull about to burn through her white face like a
thousand-watt bulb. And seeing that, seeing her there, I knew a
whole lot of things at once.

That she really was dying, either from the wizz or her disease
or the combination of the two. That she damned well knew it.
That the boy beside her was too drunk to have picked up on the
exoskeleton, but not too drunk to register the expensive jacket
and the money she had for drinks. And that what I was seeing
was exactly what it looked like.

But I couldn't add it up, right away, couldn't compute.
Something in me cringed.

And she was smiling, or anyway doing a thing she must have thought was like a smile, the expression she knew was appropriate to the situation, and nodding in time to the kid's slurred inanities, and that awful line of hers came back to me, the one about liking to watch.

And I know something now. I know that if I hadn't happened in there, hadn't seen them, I'd have been able to accept all that came later. Might even have found a way to rejoice on her behalf, or found a way to trust in whatever it is that she's since become, or had built in her image, a program that pretends to be Lise to the extent that it believes it's her. I could have believed what Rubin believes, that she was so truly past it, our hi-tech Saint Joan burning for union with that hardwired godhead in Hollywood, that nothing mattered to her except the hour of her departure. That she threw away that poor sad body with a cry of release, free of the bonds of polycarbon and hated flesh. Well, maybe, after all, she did. Maybe it was that way. I'm sure that's the way she expected it to be.

But seeing her there, that drunken kid's hand in hers, that hand she couldn't even feel, I knew, once and for all, that no human motive is ever entirely pure. Even Lise, with that corrosive, crazy drive to stardom and cybernetic immortality, had weaknesses. Was human in a way I hated myself for admitting.

She'd gone out that night, I knew, to kiss herself goodbye. To find someone drunk enough to do it for her. Because, I knew then, it was true: She did like to watch.

I think she saw me, as I left. I was practically running. If she did, I suppose she hated me worse than ever, for the horror and the pity in my face.

I never saw her again.

———

someday I'll ask Rubin why Wild Turkey sours are the only drink he knows how to make. Industrial-strength, Rubin's sours. He passes me the dented aluminum cup, while his place ticks and stirs around us with the furtive activity of his smaller creations.

"You ought to come to Frankfurt," he says again.

"Why, Rubin?"

"Because pretty soon she's going to call you up. And I think maybe you aren't ready for it. You're still screwed up about this, and it'll sound like her and think like her, and you'll get too weird behind it. Come over to Frankfurt with me and you can get a little breathing space. She won't know you're there. . . ."

"I told you," I say, remembering her at the bar in that club, "lots of work. Max—"

"Stuff Max. Max you just made rich. Max can sit on his hands. You're rich yourself, from your royalty cut on *Kings*, if you weren't too stubborn to dial up your bank account. You can afford a vacation."

I look at him and wonder when I'll tell him the story of that final glimpse. "Rubin, I appreciate it, man, but I just . . ."

He sighs, drinks. "But, what?"

"Rubin, if she calls me, is it *her*?"

He looks at me a long time. "God only knows." His cup clicks on the table. "I mean, Casey, the technology is there, so who, man, really who, is to say?"

"And you think I should come with you to Frankfurt?"

He takes off his steel-rimmed glasses and polishes them in-efficiently on the front of his plaid flannel shirt. "Yeah, I do. You need the rest. Maybe you don't need it now, but you're going to later."

"How's that?"

"When you have to edit her next release. Which will almost

certainly be soon, because she needs money bad. She's taking up a lot of ROM on some corporate mainframe, and her share of *Kings* won't come close to paying for what they had to do to put her there. And you're her editor, Casey. I mean, who else?"

And I just stare at him as he puts the glasses back on, like I can't move at all.

"Who else, man?"

And one of his constructs clicks right then, just a clear and tiny sound, and it comes to me, he's right.

Dogfight

by Michael Swanwick and William Gibson

he meant to keep on going, right down to Florida. Work passage on a gunrunner, maybe wind up conscripted into some ratass rebel army down in the war zone. Or maybe, with that ticket good as long as he didn't stop riding, he'd just never get off—Greyhound's Flying Dutchman. He grinned at his faint reflection in cold, greasy glass while the downtown lights of Norfolk slid past, the bus swaying on tired shocks as the driver slung it around a final corner. They shuddered to a halt in the terminal lot, concrete lit gray and harsh like a prison exercise yard. But Deke was watching himself starve, maybe in some snowstorm out of Oswego, with his cheek pressed up against that same bus window, and seeing his remains swept out at the next stop by a muttering old man in faded coveralls. One way or the other, he decided, it didn't mean shit to him. Except his legs seemed to have died already. And the driver called a twenty-minute stopover—Tidewater Station, Virginia. It was an old cinder-block building with two entrances to each rest room, holdover from the previous century.

Legs like wood, he made a halfhearted attempt at ghosting the notions counter, but the black girl behind it was alert, guarding the sparse contents of the old glass case as though her ass depended on it. *Probably does,* Deke thought, turning away. Opposite the washrooms, an open doorway offered GAMES, the word flickering feebly in biofluorescent plastic. He could see a

crowd of the local kickers clustered around a pool table. Aimless, his boredom following him like a cloud, he stuck his head
in. And saw a biplane, wings no longer than his thumb, blossom
bright orange flame. Corkscrewing, trailing smoke, it vanished
the instant it struck the green-felt field of the table.

"Tha's right, Tiny," a kicker bellowed, "you *take* that
sumbitch!"

"Hey," Deke said. "What's going on?"

The nearest kicker was a bean pole with a black mesh Peterbilt cap. "Tiny's defending the Max," he said, not taking his eyes
from the table.

"Oh, yeah? What's that?" But even as he asked, he saw it: a
blue enamel medal shaped like a Maltese cross, the slogan *Pour
le Mérite* divided among its arms.

The Blue Max rested on the edge of the table, directly before
a vast and perfectly immobile bulk wedged into a fragile-
looking chrome-tube chair. The man's khaki work shirt would
have hung on Deke like the folds of a sail, but it bulged across
that bloated torso so tautly that the buttons threatened to tear
away at any instant. Deke thought of southern troopers he'd
seen on his way down; of that weird, gut-heavy endotype balanced on gangly legs that looked like they'd been borrowed from
some other body. Tiny might look like that if he stood, but on a
larger scale—a forty-inch jeans inseam that would need a
woven-steel waistband to support all those pounds of swollen
gut. If Tiny were ever to stand at all—for now Deke saw that that
shiny frame was actually a wheelchair. There was something
disturbingly childlike about the man's face, an appalling suggestion of youth and even beauty in features almost buried in
fold and jowl. Embarrassed, Deke looked away. The other man,
the one standing across the table from Tiny, had bushy sideburns and a thin mouth. He seemed to be trying to push some-

thing with his eyes, wrinkles of concentration spreading from the corners. . . .

"You dumbshit or what?" The man with the Peterbilt cap turned, catching Deke's Indo proleboy denims, the brass chains at his wrists, for the first time. "Why don't you get your ass lost, fucker. Nobody wants your kind in here." He turned back to the dogfight.

Bets were being made, being covered. The kickers were producing the hard stuff, the old stuff, liberty-headed dollars and Roosevelt dimes from the stamp-and-coin stores, while more cautious bettors slapped down antique paper dollars laminated in clear plastic. Through the haze came a trio of red planes, flying in formation. Fokker D VIIs. The room fell silent. The Fokkers banked majestically under the solar orb of a two-hundred-watt bulb.

The blue Spad dove out of nowhere. Two more plunged from the shadowy ceiling, following closely. The kickers swore, and one chuckled. The formation broke wildly. One Fokker dove almost to the felt, without losing the Spad on its tail. Furiously, it zigged and zagged across the green flatlands but to no avail. At last it pulled up, the enemy hard after it, too steeply—and stalled, too low to pull out in time.

A stack of silver dimes was scooped up.

The Fokkers were outnumbered now. One had two Spads on its tail. A needle-spray of tracers tore past its cockpit. The Fokker slip-turned right, banked into an Immelmann, and was behind one of its pursuers. It fired, and the biplane fell, tumbling.

"Way to go, Tiny!" The kickers closed in around the table.

Deke was frozen with wonder. It felt like being born all over again.

———

frank's truck Stop was two miles out of town on the
Commercial Vehicles Only route. Deke had tagged it, out of idle
habit, from the bus on the way in. Now he walked back between
the traffic and the concrete crash guards. Articulated trucks
went slamming past, big eight-segmented jobs, the wash of air
each time threatening to blast him over. CVO stops were easy
makes. When he sauntered into Frank's, there was nobody to
doubt that he'd come in off a big rig, and he was able to browse
the gift shop as slowly as he liked. The wire rack with the projective wetware wafers was located between a stack of Korean
cowboy shirts and a display for Fuzz Buster mudguards. A pair
of Oriental dragons twisted in the air over the rack, either fighting or fucking, he couldn't tell which. The game he wanted was
there: a wafer labeled SPADS & FOKKERS. It took him three seconds to boost it and less time to slide the magnet—which the
cops in D.C. hadn't even bothered to confiscate—across the
universal security strip.

On the way out, he lifted two programming units and a little
Batang facilitator-remote that looked like an antique hearing aid.

he chose a highstack at random and fed the rental agent the
line he'd used since his welfare rights were yanked. Nobody ever
checked up; the state just counted occupied rooms and paid.

The cubicle smelled faintly of urine, and someone had
scrawled Hard Anarchy Liberation Front slogans across the
walls. Deke kicked trash out of a corner, sat down, back to the
wall, and ripped open the wafer pack.

There was a folded instruction sheet with diagrams of loops,
rolls, and Immelmanns, a tube of saline paste, and a computer
list of operational specs. And the wafer itself, white plastic with
a blue biplane and logo on one side, red on the other. He turned

it over and over in his hand: SPADS & FOKKERS, FOKKERS & SPADS.
Red or blue. He fitted the Batang behind his ear after coating
the inductor surface with paste, jacked its fiberoptic ribbon into
the programmer, and plugged the programmer into the wall
current. Then he slid the wafer into the programmer. It was a
cheap set, Indonesian, and the base of his skull buzzed uncomfortably as the program ran. But when it was done, a sky-blue
Spad darted restlessly through the air, a few inches from his
face. It almost glowed, it was so real. It had the strange inner life
that fanatically detailed museum-grade models often have, but
it took all of his concentration to keep it in existence. If his attention wavered at all, it lost focus, fuzzing into a pathetic blur.

He practiced until the battery in the earset died, then
slumped against the wall and fell asleep. He dreamed of flying, in a universe that consisted entirely of white clouds and
blue sky, with no up and down, and never a green field to
crash into.

he woke to a rancid smell of frying krillcakes and winced with
hunger. No cash, either. Well, there were plenty of student types
in the stack. Bound to be one who'd like to score a programming
unit. He hit the hall with the boosted spare. Not far down was a
door with a poster on it: THERE'S A HELL OF A GOOD UNIVERSE
NEXT DOOR. Under that was a starscape with a cluster of multi-
colored pills, torn from an ad for some pharmaceutical company, pasted over an inspirational shot of the "space colony"
that had been under construction since before he was born.
LET'S GO, the poster said, beneath the collaged hypnotics.

He knocked. The door opened, security slides stopping it at
a two-inch slice of girlface. "Yeah?"

"You're going to think this is stolen." He passed the programmer from hand to hand. "I mean because it's new, virtual cherry, and the bar code's still on it. But listen, I'm not gonna argue the point. No. I'm gonna let you have it for only like half what you'd pay anywhere else."

"Hey, wow, *really,* no kidding?" The visible fraction of mouth twisted into a strange smile. She extended her hand, palm up, a loose fist. Level with his chin. "Lookahere!"

There was a hole in her hand, a black tunnel that ran right up her arm. Two small red lights. Rat's eyes. They scurried toward him—growing, gleaming. Something gray streaked forward and leaped for his face.

He screamed, throwing hands up to ward it off. Legs twisting, he fell, the programmer shattering under him.

Silicate shards skittered as he thrashed, clutching his head. Where it hurt, it hurt—it hurt very badly indeed.

"Oh, my God!" Slides unsnapped, and the girl was hovering over him. "Here, listen, come on." She dangled a blue hand towel. "Grab on to this and I'll pull you up."

He looked at her through a wash of tears. Student. That fed look, the oversize sweatshirt, teeth so straight and white they could be used as a credit reference. A thin gold chain around one ankle (fuzzed, he saw, with baby-fine hair). Choppy Japanese haircut. Money. "That sucker was gonna be my dinner," he said ruefully. He took hold of the towel and let her pull him up.

She smiled but skittishly backed away from him. "Let me make it up to you," she said. "You want some food? It was only a projection, okay?"

He followed her in, wary as an animal entering a trap.

"holy shit," Deke said, "this is *real cheese.* . . ." He was sitting on a gutsprung sofa, wedged between a four-foot teddy bear and a loose stack of floppies. The room was ankle-deep in books and clothes and papers. But the food she magicked up— Gouda cheese and tinned beef and honest-to-God greenhouse wheat wafers—was straight out of the Arabian Nights.

"Hey," she said. "We know how to treat a proleboy right, huh?" Her name was Nance Bettendorf. She was seventeen. Both her parents had jobs—greedy buggers—and she was an engineering major at William and Mary. She got top marks except in English. "I guess you must really have a thing about rats. You got some kind of phobia about rats?"

He glanced sidelong at her bed. You couldn't see it, really; it was just a swell in the ground cover. "It's not like that. It just reminded me of something else, is all."

"Like what?" She squatted in front of him, the big shirt riding high up one smooth thigh.

"Well . . . did you ever see the—" his voice involuntarily rose and rushed past the words—"*Washington Monument?* Like at night? It's got these two little . . . red lights on top, aviation markers or something, and I, and I . . ." He started to shake.

"You're afraid of the Washington Monument?" Nance whooped and rolled over with laughter, long tanned legs kicking. She was wearing crimson bikini panties.

"I would die rather than look at it again," he said levelly.

She stopped laughing then, sat up, studied his face. White, even teeth worried at her lower lip, like she was dragging up something she didn't want to think about. At last she ventured, "Brainlock?"

"Yeah," he said bitterly. "They told me I'd never go back to D.C. And then the fuckers laughed."

"What did they get you for?"

"I'm a thief." He wasn't about to tell her that the actual charge was career shoplifting.

"lotta old *computer* hacks spent their lives programming machines. And you know what? The human brain is not a god-damn bit like a machine, no way. They just don't program the same." Deke knew this shrill, desperate rap, this long, circular jive that the lonely string out to the rare listener; knew it from a hundred cold and empty nights spent in the company of strangers. Nance was lost in it, and Deke, nodding and yawning, wondered if he'd even be able to stay awake when they finally hit that bed of hers.

"I built that projection I hit you with myself," she said, hug-ging her knees up beneath her chin. "It's for muggers, you know? I just happened to have it on me, and I threw it at you 'cause I thought it was so funny, you trying to sell me that shit little Indojavanese programmer." She hunched forward and held out her hand again. "Look here." Deke cringed. "No, no, it's okay, I swear it, this is different." She opened her hand.

A single blue flame danced there, perfect and ever-changing. "Look at that," she marveled. "Just look. I pro-grammed that. It's not some diddly little seven-image job either. It's a continuous two-hour loop, seven thousand, two hundred seconds, never the same twice, each instant as indi-vidual as a fucking snowflake!"

The flame's core was glacial crystal, shards and facets flash-ing up, twisting and gone, leaving behind near-subliminal im-ages so bright and sharp that they cut the eye. Deke winced. People mostly. Pretty little naked people, fucking. "How the hell did you do that?"

She rose, bare feet slipping on slick magazines, and melo-dramatically swept folds of loose printout from a raw plywood shelf. He saw a neat row of small consoles, austere and expensive-looking. Custom work. "This is the real stuff I got here. Image facilitator. Here's my fast-wipe module. This is a brainmap one-to-one function analyzer." She sang off the names like a litany. "Quantum flicker stabilizer. Program splicer. An image assembler . . ."

"You need all that to make one little flame?"

"You betcha. This is all state of the art, professional projective wetware gear. It's years ahead of anything you've seen."

"Hey," he said, "you know anything about SPADS & FOKKERS?"

She laughed. And then, because he sensed the time was right, he reached out to take her hand.

"Don't you touch me, motherfuck, don't you ever touch me!" Nance screamed, and her head slammed against the wall as she recoiled, white and shaking with terror.

"Okay!" He threw up his hands. "Okay! I'm nowhere near you. Okay?"

She cowered from him. Her eyes were round and unblinking; tears built up at the corners, rolled down ashen cheeks. Finally, she shook her head. "Hey. Deke. Sorry. I should've told you."

"Told me what?" But he had a creepy feeling . . . already knew. The way she clutched her head. The weakly spasmodic way her hands opened and closed. "You got a brainlock, too."

"Yeah." She closed her eyes. "It's a chastity lock. My asshole parents paid for it. So I can't stand to have anybody touch me or even stand too close." Eyes opened in blind hate. "I didn't even *do* anything. Not a fucking thing. But they've both got jobs and they're so horny for me to have a career that they can't piss straight. They're afraid I'd neglect my studies if I got, you know, involved in sex and stuff. The day the brainlock comes off I am going to fuck the vilest, greasiest, hairiest . . ."

She was clutching her head again. Deke jumped up and

rummaged through the medicine cabinet. He found a jar of B-complex vitamins, pocketed a few against need, and brought two to Nance, with a glass of water. "Here." He was careful to keep his distance. "This'll take the edge off."

"Yeah, yeah," she said. Then, almost to herself, "You must really think I'm a jerk."

the games room in the Greyhound station was almost empty. A lone, long-jawed fourteen-year-old was bent over a console, maneuvering rainbow fleets of submarines in the murky grid of the North Atlantic.

Deke sauntered in, wearing his new kicker drag, and leaned against a cinder-block wall made smooth by countless coats of green enamel. He'd washed the dye from his proleboy butch, boosted jeans and T-shirt from the Goodwill, and found a pair of stompers in the sauna locker of a highstack with cut-rate security.

"Seen Tiny around, friend?"

The subs darted like neon guppies. "Depends on who's asking."

Deke touched the remote behind his left ear. The Spad snap-rolled over the console, swift and delicate as a dragonfly. It was beautiful; so perfect, so *true* it made the room seem an illusion. He buzzed the grid, millimeters from the glass, taking advantage of the programmed ground effect.

The kid didn't even bother to look up. "Jackman's," he said. "Down Richmond Road, over by the surplus."

Deke let the Spad fade in midclimb.

Jackman's took up most of the third floor of an old brick building. Deke found Best Buy War Surplus first, then a broken neon sign over an unlit lobby. The sidewalk out front was lit-

tered with another kind of surplus—damaged vets, some of
them dating back to Indochina. Old men who'd left their eyes
under Asian suns squatted beside twitching boys who'd inhaled
mycotoxins in Chile. Deke was glad to have the battered elevator doors sigh shut behind him.

A dusty Dr. Pepper clock at the far side of the long, spectral
room told him it was a quarter to eight. Jackman's had been em-
balmed twenty years before he was born, sealed away behind a
yellowish film of nicotine, of polish and hair oil. Directly beneath the clock, the flat eyes of somebody's grandpappy's prize
buck regarded Deke from a framed, blown-up snapshot gone
the slick sepia of cockroach wings. There was the click and
whisper of pool, the squeak of a work boot twisting on linoleum
as a player leaned in for a shot. Somewhere high above the
green-shaded lamps hung a string of crepe-paper Christmas
bells faded to dead rose. Deke looked from one cluttered wall to
the next. No facilitator.

"Bring one in, should we need it," someone said. He
turned, meeting the mild eyes of a bald man with steel-rimmed
glasses. "My name's Cline. Bobby Earl. You don't look like you
shoot pool, mister." But there was nothing threatening in
Bobby Earl's voice or stance. He pinched the steel frames from
his nose and polished the thick lenses with a fold of tissue. He
reminded Deke of a shop instructor who'd patiently tried to
teach him retrograde biochip installation. "I'm a gambler," he
said, smiling. His teeth were white plastic. "I know I don't
much look it."

"I'm looking for Tiny," Deke said.

"Well," replacing the glasses, "you're not going to find him.
He's gone up to Bethesda to let the V.A. clean his plumbing for
him. He wouldn't fly against you any how."

"Why not?"

"Well, because you're not on the circuit or I'd know your face. You any good?" When Deke nodded, Bobby Earl called down the length of Jackman's, "Yo, Clarence! You bring out that facilitator. We got us a flyboy."

Twenty minutes later, having lost his remote and what cash he had left, Deke was striding past the broken soldiers of Best Buy.

"Now you let me tell you, boy," Bobby Earl had said in a fatherly tone as, hand on shoulder, he led Deke back to the elevator, "You're not going to win against a combat vet—you listening to me? I'm not even especially good, just an old grunt who was on hype fifteen, maybe twenty times. Ol' Tiny, he was a *pilot*. Spent his entire enlistment hyped to the gills. He's got membrane attenuation real bad . . . you ain't never going to beat him."

It was a cool night. But Deke burned with anger and humiliation.

"jesus, that's crude," Nance said as the Spad strafed mounds of pink underwear. Deke, hunched up on the couch, yanked her flashy little Braun remote from behind his ear.

"Now don't you get on my case, too, Miss rich-bitch gonna-have-a-job—"

"Hey, lighten up! It's nothing to do with you—it's just *tech*. That's a really primitive wafer you got there. I mean, on the street maybe it's fine. But compared to the work I do at school, it's—hey. You ought to let me rewrite it for you."

"Say what?"

"Lemme beef it up. These suckers are all written in hexadecimal, see, 'cause the industry programmers are all washed-out computer hacks. That's how they think. But let me take it to the reader-analyzer at the department, run a few changes on it, translate it into a modern wetlanguage. Edit out all the redundant intermediaries. That'll goose up your reaction time, cut the feedback loop in half. So you'll fly faster and better. Turn you into a real pro, Ace!" She took a hit off her bong, then doubled over laughing and choking.

"Is that legit?" Deke asked dubiously.

"Hey, why do you think people buy gold-wire remotes? For the prestige? Shit. Conductivity's better, cuts a few nanoseconds off the reaction time. And reaction time is the name of the game, kiddo."

"No," Deke said. "If it were that easy, people'd already have it. Tiny Montgomery would have it. He'd have the best."

"Don't you ever *listen*?" Nance set down the bong; brown water slopped onto the floor. "The stuff I'm working with is three years ahead of anything you'll find on the street."

"No shit," Deke said after a long pause. "I mean, you can do that?"

it was like graduating from a Model T to a ninety-three Lotus. The Spad handled like a dream, responsive to Deke's slightest thought. For weeks he played the arcades, with not a nibble. He flew against the local teens and by ones and threes shot down their planes. He took chances, played flash. And the planes tumbled. . . .

Until one day Deke was tucking his seed money away, and a lanky black straightened up from the wall. He eyed the laminateds in Deke's hand and grinned. A ruby tooth gleamed. "You know," the man said, "I *heard* there was a casper who could fly, going up against the kiddies."

———

"jesus," deke said, spreading Danish butter on a kelp stick. "I wiped the *floor* with those spades. They were good, too."

"That's nice, honey," Nance mumbled. She was working on her finals project, sweating data into a machine.

"You know, I think what's happening is I got real talent for this kind of shit. You know? I mean, the program gives me an edge, but I got the stuff to take advantage of it. I'm really getting a rep out there, you know?" Impulsively, he snapped on the radio. Scratchy Dixieland brass blared.

"Hey," Nance said. "Do you *mind*?"

"No, I'm just—" He fiddled with the knobs, came up with some slow, romantic bullshit. "There. Come on, stand up. Let's dance."

"Hey, you know I can't—"

"Sure you can, sugarcakes." He threw her the huge teddy bear and snatched up a patchwork cotton dress from the floor. He held it by the waist and sleeve, tucking the collar under his chin. It smelled of patchouli, more faintly of sweat. "See, I stand over here, you stand over there. We dance. Get it?"

Blinking softly, Nance stood and clutched the bear tightly. They danced then, slowly, staring into each other's eyes. After a while, she began to cry. But still, she was smiling.

deke was daydreaming, imagining he was Tiny Montgomery wired into his jumpjet. Imagined the machine responding to his slightest neural twitch, reflexes cranked *way* up, hype flowing steadily into his veins.

Nance's floor became jungle, her bed a plateau in the Andean foothills, and Deke flew his Spad at forced speed, as if it were a full-wired interactive combat machine. Computerized hypos fed a slow trickle of high-performance enhancement mélange into his bloodstream. Sensors were wired directly into his skull—pulling a supersonic snapturn in the green-blue bowl of sky over Bolivian rain forest. Tiny would have *felt* the airflow over control surfaces.

Below, grunts hacked through the jungle with hype-pumps strapped above elbows to give them that little extra death-dance fury in combat, a shot of liquid hell in a blue plastic vial. Maybe they got ten minutes' worth in a week. But coming in at treetop level, reflexes cranked to the max, flying so low the ground troops never spotted you until you were on them, phosgene agents released, away and gone before they could draw a bead . . . it took a constant trickle of hype just to maintain. And the direct neuron interface with the jumpjet was a two-way street. The onboard computers monitored biochemistry and decided when to open the sluice gates and give the human component a killer jolt of combat edge.

Dosages like that ate you up. Ate you good and slow and constant, etching the brain surfaces, eroding away the brain-cell membranes. If you weren't yanked from the air promptly enough, you ended up with brain-cell attenuation—with reflexes too fast for your body to handle and your fight-or-flight reflexes fucked real good. . . .

"I aced it, proleboy!"

"Hah?" Deke looked up, startled, as Nance slammed in, tossing books and bag onto the nearest heap.

"My finals project—I got exempted from exams. The prof said he'd never seen anything like it. Uh, hey, dim the lights, wouldja? The colors are weird on my eyes."

He obliged. "So show me. Show me this wunnerful thing."

"Yeah, okay." She snatched up his remote, kicked clear standing space atop the bed, and struck a pose. A spark flared into flame in her hand. It spread in a quicksilver line up her arm, around her neck, and it was a snake, with triangular head and flickering tongue. Molten colors, oranges and reds. It slithered between her breasts. "I call it a firesnake," she said proudly.

Deke leaned close, and she jerked back.

"Sorry. It's like your flame, huh? I mean, I can see these tiny little fuckers in it."

"Sort of." The firesnake flowed down her stomach. "Next month I'm going to splice two hundred separate flame programs together with meld justification in between to get the visuals. Then I'll tap the mind's body image to make it self-orienting. So it can crawl all over your body without your having to mind it. You could wear it dancing."

"Maybe I'm dumb. But if you haven't done the work yet, how come I can see it?"

Nance giggled. "That's the best part—half the work isn't done yet. Didn't have the time to assemble the pieces into a unified program. Turn on that radio, huh? I want to dance." She kicked off her shoes. Deke tuned in something gutsy. Then, at Nance's urging, turned it down, almost to a whisper.

"I scored two hits of hype, see." She was bouncing on the bed, weaving her hands like a Balinese dancer. "Ever try the stuff? In-credible. Gives you like absolute concentration. Look here." She stood *en pointe.* "Never done that before."

"Hype," Deke said. "Last person I heard of got caught with that shit got three years in the infantry. How'd you score it?"

"Cut a deal with a vet who was in grad school. She bombed out last month. Stuff gives me perfect visualization. I can hold the projection with my eyes shut. It was a snap assembling the program in my head."

"On just two hits, huh?"

"One hit. I'm saving the other. Teach was so impressed he's

sponsoring me for a job interview. A recruiter from I. G. Feuchtwaren hits campus in two weeks. That cap is gonna sell him the program *and* me. I'm gonna cut out of school two years early, straight into industry, do not pass jail, do not pay two hundred dollars."

The snake curled into a flaming tiara. It gave Deke a funny-creepy feeling to think of Nance walking out of his life.

"I'm a witch," Nance sang, "a wetware witch." She shucked her shirt over her head and sent it flying. Her fine, high breasts moved freely, gracefully, as she danced. "I'm gonna make it"—now she was singing a current pop hit—"to the . . . top!" Her nipples were small and pink and aroused. The firesnake licked at them and whipped away.

"Hey, Nance," Deke said uncomfortably. "Calm down a little, huh?"

"I'm celebrating!" She hooked a thumb into her shiny gold panties. Fire swirled around hand and crotch. "I'm the virgin goddess, baby, and I have the pow-er!" Singing again.

Deke looked away. "Gotta go now," he mumbled. Gotta go home and jerk off. He wondered where she'd hidden that second hit. Could be anywhere.

there was a protocol to the circuit, a tacit order of deference and precedence as elaborate as that of a Mandarin court. It didn't matter that Deke was hot, that his rep was spreading like wildfire. Even a name flyboy couldn't just challenge whom he wished. He had to climb the ranks. But if you flew every night. If you were always available to anybody's challenge. And if you were good . . . well, it was possible to climb fast.

Deke was one plane up. It was tournament fighting, three planes against three. Not many spectators, a dozen maybe, but it was a good fight, and they were noisy. Deke was immersed in the manic calm of combat when he realized suddenly that they had fallen silent. Saw the kickers stir and exchange glances. Eyes flicked past him. He heard the elevator doors close. Coolly, he disposed of the second of his opponent's planes, then risked a quick glance over his shoulder.

Tiny Montgomery had just entered Jackman's. The wheelchair whispered across browning linoleum, guided by tiny twitches of one imperfectly paralyzed hand. His expression was stern, blank, calm.

In that instant, Deke lost two planes. One to deresolution—gone to blur and canceled out by the facilitator—and the other because his opponent was a real fighter. Guy did a barrel roll, killing speed and slipping to the side, and strafed Deke's biplane as it shot past. It went down in flames. Their last two planes shared altitude and speed, and as they turned, trying for position, they naturally fell into a circling pattern.

The kickers made room as Tiny wheeled up against the table. Bobby Earl Cline trailed after him, lanky and casual. Deke and his opponent traded glances and pulled their machines back from the pool table so they could hear the man out. Tiny smiled. His features were small, clustered in the center of his pale, doughy face. One finger twitched slightly on the chrome handrest. "I heard about you." He looked straight at Deke. His voice was soft and shockingly sweet, a baby-girl little voice. "I heard you're good."

Deke nodded slowly. The smile left Tiny's face. His soft, fleshy lips relaxed into a natural pout, as if he were waiting for a kiss. His small, bright eyes studied Deke without malice. "Let's see what you can do, then."

Deke lost himself in the cool game of war. And when the enemy went down in smoke and flame, to explode and vanish against the table, Tiny wordlessly turned his chair, wheeled it into the elevator, and was gone.

As Deke was gathering up his winnings, Bobby Earl eased up to him and said, "The man wants to play you."

"Yeah?" Deke was nowhere near high enough on the circuit to challenge Tiny. "What's the scam?"

"Man who was coming up from Atlanta tomorrow canceled. Ol' Tiny, he was spoiling to go up against somebody new. So it looks like you get your shot at the Max."

"Tomorrow? Wednesday? Doesn't give me much prep time."

Bobby Earl smiled gently. "I don't think that makes no nevermind."

"How's that, Mr. Cline?"

"Boy, you just ain't got the *moves,* you follow me? Ain't got no surprises. You fly just like some kinda beginner, only faster and slicker. You follow what I'm trying to say?"

"I'm not sure I do. You want to put a little action on that?"

"Tell you truthful," Cline said, "I been hoping on that." He drew a small black notebook from his pocket and licked a pencil stub. "Give you five to one. They's nobody gonna give no fairer odds than that."

He looked at Deke almost sadly. "But Tiny, he's just naturally better'n you, and that's all she wrote, boy. He lives for that goddamned game, ain't *got* nothing else. Can't get out of that goddamned chair. You think you can best a man who's fighting for his life, you are just lying to yourself."

norman rockwell's portrait of the colonel regarded Deke dispassionately from the Kentucky Fried across Richmond Road from the coffee bar. Deke held his cup with hands that were cold and trembling. His skull hummed with fatigue. Cline was right, he told the colonel. I can go up against Tiny, but I can't win. The colonel stared back, gaze calm and level and not particularly kindly, taking in the coffee bar and Best Buy and all his drag-ass kingdom of Richmond Road. Waiting for Deke to admit to the terrible thing he had to do.

"The bitch is planning to leave me anyway," Deke said aloud. Which made the black countergirl look at him funny, then quickly away.

"daddy called!" Nance danced into the apartment, slamming the door behind her. "And you know what? He says if I can get this job and hold it for six months, he'll have the brain-lock reversed. Can you *believe* it? Deke?" She hesitated. "You okay?"

Deke stood. Now that the moment was on him, he felt un-real, like he was in a movie or something. "How come you never came home last night?" Nance asked.

The skin on his face was unnaturally taut, a parchment mask. "Where'd you stash the hype, Nance? I need it."

"Deke," she said, trying a tentative smile that instantly van-ished. "Deke, that's mine. My hit. I need it. For my interview."

He smiled scornfully. "You got money. You can always score another cap."

"Not by Friday! Listen, Deke, this is really important. My whole life is riding on this interview. I need that cap. It's all I got!"

"Baby, you got the fucking world! Take a look around you—six ounces of blond Lebanese hash! Little anchovy fish in tins. Unlimited medical coverage, if you need it." She was backing away from him, stumbling against the static waves of unwashed bedding and wrinkled glossy magazines that crested at the foot of her bed. "Me, I never had a glimmer of any of this. Never had the kind of edge it takes to get along. Well, this one time I am gonna. There is a match in two hours that I am going to fucking well win. Do you hear me?" He was working himself into a rage, and that was good. He needed it for what he had to do.

Nance flung up an arm, palm open, but he was ready for that and slapped her hand aside, never even catching a glimpse of the dark tunnel, let alone those little red eyes. Then they were both falling, and he was on top of her, her breath hot and rapid in his face. "Deke! Deke! I *need* that shit, Deke, my *interview*, it's the only . . . I gotta . . . gotta . . ." She twisted her face away, crying into the wall. "Please, God, please don't . . ."

"Where did you stash it?"

Pinned against the bed under his body, Nance began to spasm, her entire body convulsing in pain and fear.

"Where is it?"

Her face was bloodless, gray corpse flesh, and horror burned in her eyes. Her lips squirmed. It was too late to stop now; he'd crossed over the line. Deke felt revolted and nauseated, all the more so because on some unexpected and unwelcome level, he was *enjoying* this.

"Where is it, Nance?" And slowly, very gently, he began to stroke her face.

deke summoned Jackman's elevator with a finger that moved as fast and straight as a hornet and landed daintily as a butterfly on the call button. He was full of bouncy energy, and it was all under control. On the way up, he whipped off his shades and chuckled at his reflection in the finger-smudged chrome.

The blacks of his eyes were like pinpricks, all but invisible, and still the world was neon bright.

Tiny was waiting. The cripple's mouth turned up at the corners into a sweet smile as he took in Deke's irises, the exaggerated calm of his motions, the unsuccessful attempt to mime an undrugged clumsiness. "Well," he said in that girlish voice, "looks like I have a treat in store for me."

The Max was draped over one tube of the wheelchair. Deke took up position and bowed, not quite mockingly. "Let's fly." As challenger, he flew defense. He materialized his planes at a conservative altitude, high enough to dive, low enough to have warning when Tiny attacked. He waited.

The crowd tipped him. A fatboy with brilliantined hair looked startled, a hollow-eyed cracker started to smile. Murmurs rose. Eyes shifted slow-motion in heads frozen by hyped-up reaction time. Took maybe three nanoseconds to pinpoint the source of attack. Deke whipped his head up, and—

Sonofabitch, he was *blind!* The Fokkers were diving straight from the two-hundred-watt bulb, and Tiny had suckered him into staring right at it. His vision whited out. Deke squeezed lids tight over welling tears and frantically held visualization. He split his flight, curving two biplanes right, one left. Immediately twisting each a half-turn, then back again. He had to dodge randomly—he couldn't tell where the hostile warbirds were.

Tiny chuckled. Deke could hear him through the sounds of the crowd, the cheering and cursing and slapping down of coins that seemed to syncopate independent of the ebb and flow of the duel.

When his vision returned an instant later, a Spad was in flames and falling. Fokkers tailed his surviving planes, one on one and two on the other. Three seconds into the game and he was down one.

Dodging to keep Tiny from pinning tracers on him, he looped the single pursued plane about and drove the other toward the blind spot between Tiny and the light bulb.

Tiny's expression went very calm. The faintest shadow of disappointment—of contempt, even—was swallowed up by tranquility. He tracked the planes blandly, waiting for Deke to make his turn.

Then, just short of the blind spot, Deke shoved his Spad into a drive, the Fokkers overshooting and banking wildly to either side, twisting around to regain position.

The Spad swooped down on the third Fokker, pulled into position by Deke's other plane. Fire strafed wings and crimson fuselage. For an instant nothing happened, and Deke thought he had a fluke miss. Then the little red mother veered left and went down, trailing black, oily smoke.

Tiny frowned, small lines of displeasure marring the perfection of his mouth. Deke smiled. One even, and Tiny held position.

Both Spads were tailed closely. Deke swung them wide, and then pulled them together from opposite sides of the table. He drove them straight for each other, neutralizing Tiny's advantage . . . neither could fire without endangering his own planes. Deke cranked his machines up to top speed, slamming them at each other's nose.

An instant before they crashed, Deke sent the planes over and under one another, opening fire on the Fokkers and twisting away. Tiny was ready. Fire filled the air. Then one blue and one red plane soared free, heading in opposite directions. Behind them, two biplanes tangled in midair. Wings touched, slewed about, and the planes crumpled. They fell together, almost straight down, to the green felt below.

Ten seconds in and four planes down. A black vet pursed his lips and blew softly. Someone else shook his head in disbelief.

Tiny was sitting straight and a little forward in his wheelchair, eyes intense and unblinking, soft hands plucking feebly at the grips. None of that amused and detached bullshit now; his attention was riveted on the game. The kickers, the table, Jackman's itself, might not exist at all for him. Bobby Earl Cline laid a hand on his shoulder; Tiny didn't notice. The planes were at opposite ends of the room, laboriously gaining altitude. Deke jammed his against the ceiling, dim through the smoky haze. He spared Tiny a quick glance, and their eyes locked. Cold against cold. "Let's see your best," Deke muttered through clenched teeth.

They drove their planes together.

The hype was peaking now, and Deke could see Tiny's tracers crawling through the air between the planes. He had to put his Spad into the line of fire to get off a fair burst, then twist and bank so the Fokker's bullets would slip by his undercarriage. Tiny was every bit as hot, dodging Deke's fire and passing so close to the Spad their landing gears almost tangled as they passed.

Deke was looping his Spad in a punishingly tight turn when the hallucinations hit. The felt writhed and twisted—became the green hell of Bolivian rain forest that Tiny had flown combat over. The walls receded to gray infinity, and he felt the metal confinement of a cybernetic jumpjet close in around him.

But Deke had done his homework. He was expecting the hallucinations and knew he could deal with them. The military would never pass on a drug that couldn't be fought through. Spad and Fokker looped into another pass. He could read the tensions in Tiny Montgomery's face, the echoes of combat in deep jungle sky. They drove their planes together, feeling the torqued tensions that fed straight from instrumentation to hindbrain, the adrenaline pumps kicking in behind the armpits, the cold, fast freedom of airflow over jet-skin mingling with the smells of hot metal and fear sweat. Tracers tore past his face, and he pulled back, seeing the Spad zoom by the Fokker again, both untouched. The kickers were just going ape, waving hats and stomping feet, acting like God's own fools. Deke locked glances with Tiny again.

Malice rose up in him, and though his every nerve was taut as the carbon-crystal whiskers that kept the jumpjets from falling apart in superman turns over the Andes, he counterfeited a casual smile and winked, jerking his head slightly to one side, as if to say "Lookahere."

Tiny glanced to the side.

It was only for a fraction of a second, but that was enough. Deke pulled as fast and tight an Immelmann—right on the edge of theoretical tolerance—as had ever been seen on the circuit, and he was hanging on Tiny's tail.

Let's see you get out of this one, sucker.

Tiny rammed his plane straight down at the green, and Deke followed after. He held his fire. He had Tiny where he wanted him.

Running. Just like he'd been on his every combat mission. High on exhilaration and hype, maybe, but running scared. They were down to the felt now, flying treetop-level. Break, Deke thought, and jacked up the speed. Peripherally, he could see Bobby Earl Cline, and there was a funny look on the man's face. A pleading kind of look. Tiny's composure was shot; his face was twisted and tormented.

Now Tiny panicked and dove his plane in among the crowd. The biplanes looped and twisted between the kickers. Some jerked back involuntarily, and others laughingly swatted at them with their hands. But there was a hot glint of terror in Tiny's eyes that spoke of an eternity of fear and confinement, two edges sawing away at each other endlessly . . .

The fear was death in the air, the confinement a locking away in metal, first of the aircraft, then of the chair. Deke could read it all in his face: Combat was the only out Tiny had had, and he'd taken it every chance he got. Until some anonymous *nationalista* with an antique SAM tore him out of that blue-green Bolivian sky and slammed him straight down to Richmond Road and Jackman's and the smiling killer boy he faced this one last time across the faded cloth.

Deke rocked up on his toes, face burning with that million-dollar smile that was the trademark of the drug that had already fried Tiny before anyone ever bothered to blow him out of the sky in a hot tangle of metal and mangled flesh. It all came together then. He saw that flying was all that held Tiny together. That daily brush of fingertips against death, and then rising up from the metal coffin, alive again. He'd been holding back collapse by sheer force of will. Break that willpower, and mortality would come pouring out and drown him. Tiny would lean over and throw up in his own lap.

and deke drove it home....

There was a moment of stunned silence as Tiny's last plane vanished in a flash of light. "I did it," Deke whispered. Then, louder, "Son of a bitch, I did it!"

Across the table from him, Tiny twisted in his chair, arms jerking spastically; his head lolled over on one shoulder. Behind him, Bobby Earl Cline stared straight at Deke, his eyes hot coals.

The gambler snatched up the Max and wrapped its ribbon around a stack of laminateds. Without warning, he flung the bundle at Deke's face. Effortlessly, casually, Deke plucked it from the air.

For an instant, then, it looked like the gambler would come at him, right across the pool table. He was stopped by a tug on his sleeve. "Bobby Earl," Tiny whispered, his voice choking with humiliation, "you gotta get me . . . out of here. . . ."

Stiffly, angrily, Cline wheeled his friend around, and then away, into shadow.

Deke threw back his head and laughed. By God, he felt good! He stuffed the Max into a shirt pocket, where it hung cold and heavy. The money he crammed into his jeans. Man, he had to jump with it, his triumph leaping up through him like a wild thing, fine and strong as the flanks of a buck in the deep woods he'd seen from a Greyhound once, and for this one moment it seemed that everything was worth it somehow, all the pain and misery he'd gone through to finally win.

But Jackman's was silent. Nobody cheered. Nobody crowded around to congratulate him. He sobered, and silent, hostile faces swam into focus. Not one of these kickers was on his side. They radiated contempt, even hatred. For an interminably drawn-out moment the air trembled with potential violence . . . and then someone turned to the side, hawked up phlegm, and spat on the floor. The crowd broke up, muttering, one by one drifting into the darkness.

Deke didn't move. A muscle in one leg began to twitch, harbinger of the coming hype crash. The top of his head felt numb, and there was an awful taste in his mouth. For a second he had to hang on to the table with both hands to keep from falling down forever, into the living shadow beneath him, as he hung impaled by the prize buck's dead eyes in the photo under the Dr. Pepper clock.

A little adrenaline would pull him out of this. He needed to celebrate. To get drunk or stoned and talk it up, going over the victory time and again, contradicting himself, making up details, laughing and bragging. A starry old night like this called for big talk.

But standing there with all of Jackman's silent and vast and empty around him, he realized suddenly that he had nobody left to tell it to.

Nobody at all.

i t was hot, the night we burned Chrome. Out in the malls and plazas, moths were batting themselves to death against the neon, but in Bobby's loft the only light came from a monitor screen and the green and red LEDs on the face of the matrix simulator. I knew every chip in Bobby's simulator by heart; it looked like your workaday Ono-Sendai VII, the "Cyberspace Seven," but I'd rebuilt it so many times that you'd have had a hard time finding a square millimeter of factory circuitry in all that silicon.

We waited side by side in front of the simulator console, watching the time display in the screen's lower left corner.

"Go for it," I said, when it was time, but Bobby was already there, leaning forward to drive the Russian program into its slot with the heel of his hand. He did it with the tight grace of a kid slamming change into an arcade game, sure of winning and ready to pull down a string of free games.

A silver tide of phosphenes boiled across my field of vision as the matrix began to unfold in my head, a 3-D chessboard, infinite and perfectly transparent. The Russian program seemed to lurch as we entered the grid. If anyone else had been jacked into that part of the matrix, he might have seen a surf of flickering shadow roll out of the little yellow pyramid that represented our computer. The program was a mimetic weapon, designed to absorb local color and present itself as a crash-priority override in whatever context it encountered.

"Congratulations," I heard Bobby say. "We just became an Eastern Seaboard Fission Authority inspection probe. . . ." That meant we were clearing fiberoptic lines with the cybernetic equivalent of a fire siren, but in the simulation matrix we seemed to rush straight for Chrome's database. I couldn't see it yet, but I already knew those walls were waiting. Walls of shadow, walls of ice.

Chrome: her pretty childface smooth as steel, with eyes that would have been at home on the bottom of some deep Atlantic trench, cold gray eyes that lived under terrible pressure. They said she cooked her own cancers for people who crossed her, rococo custom variations that took years to kill you. They said a lot of things about Chrome, none of them at all reassuring.

So I blotted her out with a picture of Rikki. Rikki kneeling in a shaft of dusty sunlight that slanted into the loft through a grid of steel and glass: her faded camouflage fatigues, her translucent rose sandals, the good line of her bare back as she rummaged through a nylon gear bag. She looks up, and a half-blond curl falls to tickle her nose. Smiling, buttoning an old shirt of Bobby's, frayed khaki cotton drawn across her breasts.

She smiles.

"Son of a bitch," said Bobby, "we just told Chrome we're an IRS audit and three Supreme Court subpoenas. . . . Hang on to your ass, Jack. . . ."

So long, Rikki. Maybe now I see you never.

And dark, so dark, in the halls of Chrome's ice.

bobby was a cowboy, and ice was the nature of his game, *ice* from ICE, Intrusion Countermeasures Electronics. The matrix is an abstract representation of the relationships between data systems. Legitimate programmers jack into their employers' sector of the matrix and find themselves surrounded by bright geometries representing the corporate data.

Towers and fields of it ranged in the colorless nonspace of the simulation matrix, the electronic consensus-hallucination that facilitates the handling and exchange of massive quantities of data. Legitimate programmers never see the walls of ice they work behind, the walls of shadow that screen their operations from others, from industrial-espionage artists and hustlers like Bobby Quine.

Bobby was a cowboy. Bobby was a cracksman, a burglar, casing mankind's extended electronic nervous system, rustling data and credit in the crowded matrix, monochrome nonspace where the only stars are dense concentrations of information, and high above it all burn corporate galaxies and the cold spiral arms of military systems.

Bobby was another one of those young-old faces you see drinking in the Gentleman Loser, the chic bar for computer cowboys, rustlers, cybernetic second-story men. We were partners.

Bobby Quine and Automatic Jack. Bobby's the thin, pale dude with the dark glasses, and Jack's the mean-looking guy with the myoelectric arm. Bobby's software and Jack's hard; Bobby punches console and Jack runs down all the little things that can give you an edge. Or, anyway, that's what the scene watchers in the Gentleman Loser would've told you, before Bobby decided to burn Chrome. But they also might've told you that Bobby was losing his edge, slowing down. He was twenty-eight, Bobby, and that's old for a console cowboy.

Both of us were good at what we did, but somehow that one big score just wouldn't come down for us. I knew where to go for the right gear, and Bobby had all his licks down pat. He'd sit back with a white terry sweatband across his forehead and whip moves on those keyboards faster than you could follow, punching his way through some of the fanciest ice in the business, but that was when something happened that managed to get him totally wired, and that didn't happen often. Not highly motivated, Bobby, and I was the kind of guy who's happy to have the rent covered and a clean shirt to wear.

But Bobby had this thing for girls, like they were his private tarot or something, the way he'd get himself moving. We never talked about it, but when it started to look like he was losing his touch that summer, he started to spend more time in the Gentleman Loser. He'd sit at a table by the open doors and watch the crowd slide by, nights when the bugs were at the neon and the air smelled of perfume and fast food. You could see his sunglasses scanning those faces as they passed, and he must have decided that Rikki's was the one he was waiting for, the wild card and the luck changer. The new one.

i went to New York to check out the market, to see what was available in hot software.

The Finn's place has a defective hologram in the window, METRO HOLOGRAFIX, over a display of dead flies wearing fur coats of gray dust. The scrap's waist-high, inside, drifts of it rising to meet walls that are barely visible behind nameless junk, behind sagging pressboard shelves stacked with old skin magazines and yellow-spined years of *National Geographic*.

"You need a gun," said the Finn. He looks like a recombo DNA project aimed at tailoring people for high-speed burrowing. "You're in luck. I got the new Smith and Wesson, the four-oh-eight Tactical. Got this xenon projector slung under the barrel, see, batteries in the grip, throw you a twelve-inch high-noon circle in the pitch dark at fifty yards. The light source is so narrow, it's almost impossible to spot. It's just like voodoo in a nightfight."

I let my arm clunk down on the table and started the fingers drumming; the servos in the hand began whining like over-worked mosquitoes. I knew that the Finn really hated the sound.

"You looking to pawn that?" He prodded the Duralumin wrist joint with the chewed shaft of a felt-tip pen. "Maybe get yourself something a little quieter?"

I kept it up. "I don't need any guns, Finn."

"Okay," he said, "okay," and I quit drumming. "I only got this one item, and I don't even know what it is." He looked un-happy. "I got it off these bridge-and-tunnel kids from Jersey last week."

"So when'd you ever buy anything you didn't know what it was, Finn?"

"Wise ass." And he passed me a transparent mailer with something in it that looked like an audio cassette through the bubble padding. "They had a passport," he said. "They had credit cards and a watch. And that."

"They had the contents of somebody's pockets, you mean."

He nodded. "The passport was Belgian. It was also bogus, looked to me, so I put it in the furnace. Put the cards in with it. The watch was okay, a Porsche, nice watch."

It was obviously some kind of plug-in military program. Out of the mailer, it looked like the magazine of a small assault rifle, coated with nonreflective black plastic. The edges and corners showed bright metal; it had been knocking around for a while.

"I'll give you a bargain on it, Jack. For old times' sake."

I had to smile at that. Getting a bargain from the Finn was like God repealing the law of gravity when you have to carry a heavy suitcase down ten blocks of airport corridor.

"Looks Russian to me," I said. "Probably the emergency sewage controls for some Leningrad suburb. Just what I need."

"You know," said the Finn. "I got a pair of shoes older than you are. Sometimes I think you got about as much class as those yahoos from Jersey. What do you want me to tell you, it's the keys to the Kremlin? You figure out what the goddamn thing is. Me, I just sell the stuff."

I bought it.

bodiless, we swerve into Chrome's castle of ice. And we're fast, fast. It feels like we're surfing the crest of the invading program, hanging ten above the seething glitch systems as they mutate. We're sentient patches of oil swept along down corridors of shadow.

Somewhere we have bodies, very far away, in a crowded loft roofed with steel and glass. Somewhere we have microseconds, maybe time left to pull out.

We've crashed her gates disguised as an audit and three subpoenas, but her defenses are specifically geared to cope with that kind of official intrusion. Her most sophisticated ice is structured to fend off warrants, writs, subpoenas. When we breached the first gate, the bulk of her data vanished behind core-command ice, these walls we see as leagues of corridor, mazes of shadow. Five separate landlines spurted May Day signals to law firms, but the virus had already taken over the parameter ice. The glitch systems gobble the distress calls as our mimetic subprograms scan anything that hasn't been blanked by core command.

The Russian program lifts a Tokyo number from the unscreened data, choosing it for frequency of calls, average length of calls, the speed with which Chrome returned those calls.

"Okay," says Bobby, "we're an incoming scrambler call from a pal of hers in Japan. That should help."

Ride 'em, cowboy.

bobby read his future in women; his girls were omens, changes in the weather, and he'd sit all night in the Gentleman Loser, waiting for the season to lay a new face down in front of him like a card.

I was working late in the loft one night, shaving down a chip, my arm off and the little waldo jacked straight into the stump.

Bobby came in with a girl I hadn't seen before, and usually I feel a little funny if a stranger sees me working that way, with those leads clipped to the hard carbon studs that stick out of my stump. She came right over and looked at the magnified image on the screen, then saw the waldo moving under its vacuum-sealed dust cover. She didn't say anything, just watched. Right away I had a good feeling about her; it's like that sometimes.

"Automatic Jack, Rikki. My associate."

He laughed, put his arm around her waist, something in his tone letting me know that I'd be spending the night in a dingy room in a hotel.

"Hi," she said. Tall, nineteen or maybe twenty, and she definitely had the goods. With just those few freckles across the bridge of her nose and eyes somewhere between dark amber and French coffee. Tight black jeans rolled to midcalf and a narrow plastic belt that matched the rose-colored sandals.

But now when I see her sometimes when I'm trying to sleep, I see her somewhere out on the edge of all this sprawl of cities and smoke, and it's like she's a hologram stuck behind my eyes, in a bright dress she must've worn once, when I knew her, something that doesn't quite reach her knees. Bare legs long and straight. Brown hair, streaked with blond, hoods her face, blown in a wind from somewhere, and I see her wave goodbye.

Bobby was making a show of rooting through a stack of audio cassettes. "I'm on my way, cowboy," I said, unclipping the waldo. She watched attentively as I put my arm back on.

"Can you fix things?" she asked.

"Anything, anything you want, Automatic Jack'll fix it." I snapped my Duralumin fingers for her.

She took a little simstim deck from her belt and showed me the broken hinge on the cassette cover.

"Tomorrow," I said, "no problem."

And my oh my, I said to myself, sleep pulling me down the six flights to the street, *what'll Bobby's luck be like with a fortune cookie like that? If his system worked, we'd be striking it rich any night now.* In the street I grinned and yawned and waved for a cab.

chrome's castle is dissolving, sheets of ice shadow flickering and fading, eaten by the glitch systems that spin out from the Russian program, tumbling away from our central logic thrust and infecting the fabric of the ice itself. The glitch systems are cybernetic virus analogs, self-replicating and voracious. They mutate constantly, in unison, subverting and absorbing Chrome's defenses.

Have we already paralyzed her, or is a bell ringing somewhere, a red light blinking? Does she know?

rikki wildside, Bobby called her, and for those first few weeks it must have seemed to her that she had it all, the whole teeming show spread out for her, sharp and bright under the neon. She was new to the scene, and she had all the miles of malls and plazas to prowl, all the shops and clubs, and Bobby to explain the wild side, the tricky wiring on the dark underside of things, all the players and their names and their games. He made her feel at home.

"What happened to your arm?" she asked me one night in the Gentleman Loser, the three of us drinking at a small table in a corner.

"Hang-gliding," I said, "accident."

"Hang-gliding over a wheatfield," said Bobby, "place called Kiev. Our Jack's just hanging there in the dark, under a Nightwing parafoil, with fifty kilos of radar jammed between his legs, and some Russian asshole accidentally burns his arm off with a laser."

I don't remember how I changed the subject, but I did.

I was still telling myself that it wasn't Rikki who was getting to me, but what Bobby was doing with her. I'd known him for a long time, since the end of the war, and I knew he used women as counters in a game, Bobby Quine versus fortune, versus time and the night of cities. And Rikki had turned up just when he needed something to get him going, something to aim for. So he'd set her up as a symbol for everything he wanted and couldn't have, everything he'd had and couldn't keep.

I didn't like having to listen to him tell me how much he loved her, and knowing he believed it only made it worse. He was a past master at the hard fall and the rapid recovery, and I'd seen it happen a dozen times before. He might as well have had NEXT printed across his sunglasses in green Day-Glo capitals, ready to flash out at the first interesting face that flowed past the tables in the Gentleman Loser.

I knew what he did to them. He turned them into emblems, sigils on the map of his hustler's life, navigation beacons he could follow through a sea of bars and neon. What else did he have to steer by? He didn't love money, in and of itself, not enough to follow its lights. He wouldn't work for power over other people; he hated the responsibility it brings. He had some basic pride in his skill, but that was never enough to keep him pushing.

So he made do with women.

When Rikki showed up, he needed one in the worst way. He was fading fast, and smart money was already whispering that the edge was off his game. He needed that one big score, and soon, because he didn't know any other kind of life, and all his clocks were set for hustler's time, calibrated in risk and adrenaline and that supernal dawn calm that comes when every move's proved right and a sweet lump of someone else's credit clicks into your own account.

It was time for him to make his bundle and get out; so Rikki got set up higher and farther away than any of the others ever had, even though—and I felt like screaming it at him—she was right there, alive, totally real, human, hungry, resilient, bored, beautiful, excited, all the things she was. . . .

Then he went out one afternoon, about a week before I made the trip to New York to see Finn. Went out and left us there in the loft, waiting for a thunderstorm. Half the skylight was shadowed by a dome they'd never finished, and the other half showed sky, black and blue with clouds. I was standing by the bench, looking up at that sky, stupid with the hot afternoon, the humidity, and she touched me, touched my shoulder, the half-inch border of taut pink scar that the arm doesn't cover. Anybody else ever touched me there, they went on to the shoulder, the neck. . . .

But she didn't do that. Her nails were lacquered black, not pointed, but tapered oblongs, the lacquer only a shade darker than the carbon-fiber laminate that sheaths my arm. And her hand went down the arm, black nails tracing a weld in the laminate, down to the black anodized elbow joint, out to the wrist, her hand soft-knuckled as a child's, fingers spreading to lock over mine, her palm against the perforated Duralumin.

Her other palm came up to brush across the feedback pads, and it rained all afternoon, raindrops drumming on the steel and soot-stained glass above Bobby's bed.

ice walls flick away like supersonic butterflies made of shade. Beyond them, the matrix's illusion of infinite space. It's like watching a tape of a prefab building going up; only the tape's reversed and run at high speed, and these walls are torn wings.

Trying to remind myself that this place and the gulfs beyond are only representations, that we aren't "in" Chrome's computer, but interfaced with it, while the matrix simulator in Bobby's loft generates this illusion . . . The core data begin to emerge, exposed, vulnerable. . . . This is the far side of ice, the view of the matrix I've never seen before, the view that fifteen million legitimate console operators see daily and take for granted.

The core data tower around us like vertical freight trains, color-coded for access. Bright primaries, impossibly bright in that transparent void, linked by countless horizontals in nursery blues and pinks.

But ice still shadows something at the center of it all: the heart of all Chrome's expensive darkness, the very heart . . .

it was late afternoon when I got back from my shopping expedition to New York. Not much sun through the skylight, but an ice pattern glowed on Bobby's monitor screen, a 2-D graphic representation of someone's computer defenses, lines of neon woven like an Art Deco prayer rug. I turned the console off, and the screen went completely dark.

Rikki's things were spread across my workbench, nylon bags spilling clothes and makeup, a pair of bright red cowboy boots, audio cassettes, glossy Japanese magazines about simstim stars. I stacked it all under the bench and then took my arm off, forgetting that the program I'd brought from the Finn was in the righthand pocket of my jacket, so that I had to fumble it out left-handed and then get it into the padded jaws of the jeweler's vise.

The waldo looks like an old audio turntable, the kind that played disc records, with the vise set up under a transparent dust cover. The arm itself is just over a centimeter long, swinging out on what would've been the tone arm on one of those turntables. But I don't look at that when I've clipped the leads to my stump; I look at the scope, because that's my arm there in black and white, magnification 40 x.

I ran a tool check and picked up the laser. It felt a little heavy; so I scaled my weight-sensor input down to a quarter-kilo per gram and got to work. At 40 x the side of the program looked like a trailer truck.

It took eight hours to crack: three hours with the waldo and the laser and four dozen taps, two hours on the phone to a contact in Colorado, and three hours to run down a lexicon disc that could translate eight-year-old technical Russian.

Then Cyrillic alphanumerics started reeling down the monitor, twisting themselves into English halfway down. There were a lot of gaps, where the lexicon ran up against specialized military acronyms in the readout I'd bought from my man in Colorado, but it did give me some idea of what I'd bought from the Finn.

I felt like a punk who'd gone out to buy a switchblade and come home with a small neutron bomb.

Screwed again, I thought. *What good's a neutron bomb in a streetfight?* The thing under the dust cover was right out of my league. I didn't even know where to unload it, where to look for a buyer. Someone had, but he was dead, someone with a Porsche watch and a fake Belgian passport, but I'd never tried to move in those circles. The Finn's muggers from the 'burbs had knocked over someone who had some highly arcane connections.

The program in the jeweler's vise was a Russian military ice-breaker, a killer-virus program.

It was dawn when Bobby came in alone. I'd fallen asleep with a bag of takeout sandwiches in my lap.

"You want to eat?" I asked him, not really awake, holding out my sandwiches. I'd been dreaming of the program, of its waves of hungry glitch systems and mimetic subprograms; in the dream it was an animal of some kind, shapeless and flowing.

He brushed the bag aside on his way to the console, punched a function key. The screen lit with the intricate pattern I'd seen there that afternoon. I rubbed sleep from my eyes with my left hand, one thing I can't do with my right. I'd fallen asleep trying to decide whether to tell him about the program. Maybe I should try to sell it alone, keep the money, go somewhere new, ask Rikki to go with me.

"Whose is it?" I asked.

He stood there in a black cotton jump suit, an old leather jacket thrown over his shoulders like a cape. He hadn't shaved for a few days, and his face looked thinner than usual.

"It's Chrome's," he said.

My arm convulsed, started clicking, fear translated to the myoelectrics through the carbon studs. I spilled the sandwiches; limp sprouts, and bright yellow dairy-produce slices on the unswept wooden floor.

"You're stone crazy," I said.

"No," he said, "you think she rumbled it? No way. We'd be dead already. I locked on to her through a triple-blind rental system in Mombasa and an Algerian comsat. She knew somebody was having a look-see, but she couldn't trace it."

If Chrome had traced the pass Bobby had made at her ice, we were good as dead. But he was probably right, or she'd have had me blown away on my way back from New York. "Why her, Bobby? Just give me one reason. . . ."

Chrome: I'd seen her maybe half a dozen times in the Gentleman Loser. Maybe she was slumming, or checking out the human condition, a condition she didn't exactly aspire to. A sweet little heart-shaped face framing the nastiest pair of eyes you ever saw. She'd looked fourteen for as long as anyone could remember, hyped out of anything like a normal metabolism on some massive program of serums and hormones. She was as ugly a customer as the street ever produced, but she didn't belong to the street anymore. She was one of the Boys, Chrome, a member in good standing of the local Mob subsidary. Word was, she'd gotten started as a dealer, back when synthetic pituitary hormones were still proscribed. But she hadn't had to move hormones for a long time. Now she owned the House of Blue Lights.

"You're flat-out crazy, Quine. You give me one sane reason for having that stuff on your screen. You ought to dump it, and I mean *now*. . . ."

"Talk in the Loser," he said, shrugging out of the leather jacket. "Black Myron and Crow Jane. Jane, she's up on all the sex lines, claims she knows where the money goes. So she's arguing with Myron that Chrome's the controlling interest in the Blue Lights, not just some figurehead for the Boys."

" 'The Boys,' Bobby," I said. "That's the operative word there. You still capable of seeing that? We don't mess with the Boys, remember? That's why we're still walking around."

"That's why we're still poor, partner." He settled back into the swivel chair in front of the console, unzipped his jump suit, and scratched his skinny white chest. "But maybe not for much longer."

"I think maybe this partnership just got itself permanently dissolved."

Then he grinned at me. The grin was truly crazy, feral and focused, and I knew that right then he really didn't give a shit about dying.

"Look," I said, "I've got some money left, you know? Why don't you take it and get the tube to Miami, catch a hopper to Montego Bay. You need a rest, man. You've got to get your act together."

"My act, Jack," he said, punching something on the keyboard, "never has been this together before." The neon prayer rug on the screen shivered and woke as an animation program cut in, ice lines weaving with hypnotic frequency, a living mandala. Bobby kept punching, and the movement slowed; the pattern resolved itself, grew slightly less complex, became an alternation between two distant configurations. A first-class piece of work, and I hadn't thought he was still that good. "Now," he said, "there, see it? Wait. There. There again. And there. Easy to miss. That's it. Cuts in every hour and twenty minutes with a squirt transmission to their comsat. We could live for a year on what she pays them weekly in negative interest."

"Whose comsat?"

"Zürich. Her bankers. That's her bankbook, Jack. That's where the money goes. Crow Jane was right."

I stood there. My arm forgot to click.

"So how'd you do in New York, partner? You get anything that'll help me cut ice? We're going to need whatever we can get."

I kept my eyes on his, forced myself not to look in the direction of the waldo, the jeweler's vise. The Russian program was there, under the dust cover.

Wild cards, luck changers.

"Where's Rikki?" I asked him, crossing to the console, pretending to study the alternating patterns on the screen.

"Friends of hers," he shrugged, "kids, they're all into simstim." He smiled absently. "I'm going to do it for her, man."

"I'm going out to think about this, Bobby. You want me to come back, you keep your hands off the board."

"I'm doing it for her," he said as the door closed behind me. "You know I am."

and down now, down, the program a roller coaster through this fraying maze of shadow walls, gray cathedral spaces between the bright towers. Headlong speed.

Black ice. Don't think about it. Black ice.

Too many stories in the Gentleman Loser; black ice is a part of the mythology. Ice that kills. Illegal, but then aren't we all? Some kind of neural-feedback weapon, and you connect with it only once. Like some hideous Word that eats the mind from the inside out. Like an epileptic spasm that goes on and on until there's nothing left at all . . .

And we're diving for the floor of Chrome's shadow castle.

Trying to brace myself for the sudden stopping of breath, a sickness and final slackening of the nerves. Fear of that cold Word waiting, down there in the dark.

———

i went out and looked for Rikki, found her in a café with a boy with Sendai eyes, half-healed suture lines radiating from his bruised sockets. She had a glossy brochure spread open on the table, Tally Isham smiling up from a dozen photographs, the Girl with the Zeiss Ikon Eyes.

Her little simstim deck was one of the things I'd stacked under my bench the night before, the one I'd fixed for her the day after I'd first seen her. She spent hours jacked into that unit, the contact band across her forehead like a gray plastic tiara. Tally Isham was her favorite, and with the contact band on, she was gone, off somewhere in the recorded sensorium of sim-stim's biggest star. Simulated stimuli: the world—all the inter-esting parts, anyway—as perceived by Tally Isham. Tally raced a black Fokker ground-effect plane across Arizona mesa tops. Tally dived the Truk Island preserves. Tally partied with the su-perrich on private Greek islands, heartbreaking purity of those tiny white seaports at dawn.

Actually she looked a lot like Tally, same coloring and cheek-bones. I thought Rikki's mouth was stronger. More sass. She didn't want to *be* Tally Isham, but she coveted the job. That was her ambition, to be in simstim. Bobby just laughed it off. She talked to me about it, though. "How'd I look with a pair of these?" she'd ask, holding a full-page headshot, Tally Isham's blue Zeiss Ikons lined up with her own amber-brown. She'd had her corneas done twice, but she still wasn't 20-20; so she wanted Ikons. Brand of the stars. Very expensive.

"You still window-shopping for eyes?" I asked as I sat down.

"Tiger just got some," she said. She looked tired, I thought.

Tiger was so pleased with his Sendais that he couldn't help smiling, but I doubted whether he'd have smiled otherwise. He had the kind of uniform good looks you get after your seventh trip to the surgical boutique; he'd probably spend the rest of his life looking vaguely like each new season's media front-runner; not too obvious a copy, but nothing too original, either.

"Sendai, right?" I smiled back.

He nodded. I watched as he tried to take me in with his idea of a professional, simstim glance. He was pretending that he was recording. I thought he spent too long on my arm. "They'll be great on peripherals when the muscles heal," he said, and I saw how carefully he reached for his double espresso. Sendai eyes are notorious for depth-perception defects and warranty hassles, among other things.

"Tiger's leaving for Hollywood tomorrow."

"Then maybe Chiba City, right?" I smiled at him. He didn't smile back. "Got an offer, Tiger? Know an agent?"

"Just checking it out," he said quietly. Then he got up and left. He said a quick goodbye to Rikki, but not to me.

"That kid's optic nerves may start to deteriorate inside six months. You know that, Rikki? Those Sendais are illegal in England, Denmark, lots of places. You can't replace nerves."

"Hey, Jack, no lectures." She stole one of my croissants and nibbled at the top of one of its horns.

"I thought I was your adviser, kid."

"Yeah. Well, Tiger's not too swift, but everybody knows about Sendais. They're all he can afford. So he's taking a chance. If he gets work, he can replace them."

"With these?" I tapped the Zeiss Ikon brochure. "Lot of money, Rikki. You know better than to take a gamble like that."

She nodded. "I want Ikons."

"If you're going up to Bobby's tell him to sit tight until he hears from me."

"Sure. It's business?"

"Business," I said. But it was craziness.

I drank my coffee, and she ate both my croissants. Then I walked her down to Bobby's. I made fifteen calls, each one from a different pay phone.

Business. Bad craziness.

All in all, it took us six weeks to set the burn up, six weeks of Bobby telling me how much he loved her. I worked even harder, trying to get away from that.

Most of it was phone calls. My fifteen initial and very oblique inquiries each seemed to breed fifteen more. I was looking for a certain service Bobby and I both imagined as a requisite part of the world's clandestine economy, but which probably never had more than five customers at a time. It would be one that never advertised.

We were looking for the world's heaviest fence, for a non-aligned money laundry capable of dry-cleaning a megabuck on-line cash transfer and then forgetting about it.

All those calls were a waste, finally, because it was the Finn who put me on to what we needed. I'd gone up to New York to buy a new blackbox rig, because we were going broke paying for all those calls.

I put the problem to him as hypothetically as possible.

"Macao," he said.

"Macao?"

"The Long Hum family. Stockbrokers."

He even had the number. You want a fence, ask another fence.

The Long Hum people were so oblique that they made my idea of a subtle approach look like a tactical nuke-out. Bobby had to make two shuttle runs to Hong Kong to get the deal straight. We were running out of capital, and fast. I still don't know why I decided to go along with it in the first place; I was scared of Chrome, and I'd never been all that hot to get rich.

I tried telling myself that it was a good idea to burn the House of Blue Lights because the place was a creep joint, but I just couldn't buy it. I didn't like the Blue Lights, because I'd spent a supremely depressing evening there once, but that was no excuse for going after Chrome. Actually I halfway assumed we were going to die in the attempt. Even with that killer program, the odds weren't exactly in our favor.

Bobby was lost in writing the set of commands we were going to plug into the dead center of Chrome's computer. That was going to be my job because Bobby was going to have his hands full trying to keep the Russian program from going straight for the kill. It was too complex for us to rewrite, and so he was going to try to hold it back for the two seconds I needed.

I made a deal with a streetfighter named Miles. He was going to follow Rikki the night of the burn, keep her in sight, and phone me at a certain time. If I wasn't there, or didn't answer in just a certain way, I'd told him to grab her and put her on the first tube out. I gave him an envelope to give her, money and a note.

Bobby really hadn't thought about that, much, how things would go for her if we blew it. He just kept telling me he loved her, where they were going to go together, how they'd spend the money.

"Buy her a pair of Ikons first, man. That's what she wants. She's serious about that simstim scene."

"Hey," he said, looking up from the keyboard, "she won't need to work. We're going to make it, Jack. She's my luck. She won't ever have to work again."

"Your luck," I said. I wasn't happy. I couldn't remember when I had been happy. "You seen your luck around lately?"

He hadn't, but neither had I. We'd both been too busy.

I missed her. Missing her reminded me of my one night in

the House of Blue Lights, because I'd gone there out of missing someone else. I'd gotten drunk to begin with, then I'd started hitting Vasopressin inhalers. If your main squeeze has just decided to walk out on you, booze and Vasopressin are the ultimate in masochistic pharmacology; the juice makes you maudlin and the Vasopressin makes you remember, I mean really remember. Clinically they use the stuff to counter senile amnesia, but the street finds its own uses for things. So I'd bought myself an ultraintense replay of a bad affair; trouble is, you get the bad with the good. Go gunning for transports of animal ecstasy and you get what you said, too, and what she said to that, how she walked away and never looked back.

I don't remember deciding to go to the Blue Lights, or how I got there, hushed corridors and this really tacky decorative waterfall trickling somewhere, or maybe just a hologram of one. I had a lot of money that night; somebody had given Bobby a big roll for opening a three-second window in someone else's ice.

I don't think the crew on the door liked my looks, but I guess my money was okay.

I had more to drink there when I'd done what I went there for. Then I made some crack to the barman about closet necrophiliacs, and that didn't go down too well. Then this very large character insisted on calling me War Hero, which I didn't like. I think I showed him some tricks with the arm, before the lights went out, and I woke up two days later in a basic sleeping module somewhere else. A cheap place, not even room to hang yourself. And I sat there on that narrow foam slab and cried.

Some things are worse than being alone. But the thing they sell in the House of Blue Lights is so popular that it's almost legal.

———

at the heart of darkness, the still center, the glitch systems shred the dark with whirlwinds of light, translucent razors spinning away from us; we hang in the center of a silent slow-motion explosion, ice fragments falling away forever, and Bobby's voice comes in across light-years of electronic void illusion—

"Burn the bitch down. I can't hold the thing back—"

The Russian program, rising through towers of data, blotting out the playroom colors. And I plug Bobby's homemade command package into the center of Chrome's cold heart. The squirt transmission cuts in, a pulse of condensed information that shoots straight up, past the thickening tower of darkness, the Russian program, while Bobby struggles to control that crucial second. An unformed arm of shadow twitches from the towering dark, too late.

We've done it.

The matrix folds itself around me like an origami trick.

And the loft smells of sweat and burning circuitry.

I thought I heard Chrome scream, a raw metal sound, but I couldn't have.

bobby was laughing, tears in his eyes. The elapsed-time figure in the corner of the monitor read 07:24:05. The burn had taken a little under eight minutes.

And I saw that the Russian program had melted in its slot.

We'd given the bulk of Chrome's Zürich account to a dozen world charities. There was too much there to move, and we knew we had to break her, burn her straight down, or she might come after us. We took less than ten percent for ourselves and shot it through the Long Hum setup in Macao. They took sixty percent of that for themselves and kicked what was left back to us through the most convoluted sector of the Hong Kong exchange. It took an hour before our money started to reach the two accounts we'd opened in Zürich.

I watched zeros pile up behind a meaningless figure on the monitor. I was rich.

Then, the phone rang. It was Miles. I almost blew the code phrase.

"Hey, Jack, man, I dunno—what's it all about, with this girl of yours? Kinda funny thing here . . ."

"What? Tell me."

"I been on her, like you said, tight but out of sight. She goes to the Loser, hangs out, then she gets a tube. Goes to the House of Blue Lights—"

"She what?"

"Side door. *Employees* only. No way I could get past their security."

"Is she there now?"

"No, man, I just lost her. It's insane down here, like the Blue Lights just shut down, looks like for good, seven kinds of alarms going off, everybody running, the heat out in riot gear . . . Now there's all this stuff going on, insurance guys, real-estate types, vans with municipal plates. . . ."

"Miles, where'd she go?"

"Lost her, Jack."

"Look, Miles, you keep the money in the envelope, right?"

"You serious? Hey, I'm real sorry. I—"

I hung up.

"Wait'll we tell her," Bobby was saying, rubbing a towel across his bare chest.

"You tell her yourself, cowboy. I'm going for a walk."

So I went out into the night and the neon and let the crowd pull me along, walking blind, willing myself to be just a segment of that mass organism, just one more drifting chip of consciousness under the geodesics. I didn't think, just put one foot in front of another, but after a while I did think, and it all made sense. She'd needed the money.

I thought about Chrome, too. That we'd killed her, murdered her, as surely as if we'd slit her throat. The night that carried me along through the malls and plazas would be hunting her now, and she had nowhere to go. How many enemies would she have in this crowd alone? How many would move, now they weren't held back by fear of her money? We'd taken her for everything she had. She was back on the street again. I doubted she'd live till dawn.

Finally I remembered the café, the one where I'd met Tiger.

Her sunglasses told the whole story, huge black shades with a telltale smudge of fleshtone paintstick in the corner of one lens. "Hi, Rikki," I said, and I was ready when she took them off.

Blue, Tally Isham blue. The clear trademark blue they're famous for, ZEISS IKON ringing each iris in tiny capitals, the letters suspended there like flecks of gold.

"They're beautiful," I said. Paintstick covered the bruising. No scars with work that good. "You made some money."

"Yeah, I did." Then she shivered. "But I won't make any more, not that way."

"I think that place is out of business."

"Oh." Nothing moved in her face then. The new blue eyes were still and very deep.

"It doesn't matter. Bobby's waiting for you. We just pulled down a big score."

"No. I've got to go. I guess he won't understand, but I've got to go."

I nodded, watching the arm swing up to take her hand; it didn't seem to be part of me at all, but she held on to it like it was.

"I've got a one-way ticket to Hollywood. Tiger knows some people I can stay with. Maybe I'll even get to Chiba City."

She was right about Bobby. I went back with her. He didn't understand. But she'd already served her purpose, for Bobby, and I wanted to tell her not to hurt for him, because I could see that she did. He wouldn't even come out into the hallway after she had packed her bags. I put the bags down and kissed her and messed up the paintstick, and something came up inside me the way the killer program had risen above Chrome's data. A sudden stopping of the breath, in a place where no word is. But she had a plane to catch.

Bobby was slumped in the swivel chair in front of his monitor, looking at his string of zeros. He had his shades on, and I knew he'd be in the Gentleman Loser by nightfall, checking out the weather, anxious for a sign, someone to tell him what his new life would be like. I couldn't see it being very different. More comfortable, but he'd always be waiting for that next card to fall.

I tried not to imagine her in the House of Blue Lights, working three-hour shifts in an approximation of REM sleep, while her body and a bundle of conditioned reflexes took care of business. The customers never got to complain that she was faking it, because those were real orgasms. But she felt them, if she felt them at all, as faint silver flares somewhere out on the edge of sleep. Yeah, it's so popular, it's almost legal. The customers are torn between needing someone and wanting to be alone at the same time, which has probably always been the name of that particular game, even before we had the neuroelectronics to enable them to have it both ways.

I picked up the phone and punched the number for her airline. I gave them her real name, her flight number. "She's changing that," I said, "to Chiba City. That's right. Japan." I thumbed my credit card into the slot and punched my ID code. "First class." Distant hum as they scanned my credit records. "Make that a return ticket."

But I guess she cashed the return fare, or else didn't need it, because she hasn't come back. And sometimes late at night I'll pass a window with posters of simstim stars, all those beautiful, identical eyes staring back at me out of faces that are nearly as identical, and sometimes the eyes are hers, but none of the faces are, none of them ever are, and I see her far out on the edge of all this sprawl of night and cities, and then she waves goodbye.